WILDERNESS #6

BLACK POWDER JUSTICE

DAVID THOMPSON

LEISURE BOOKS NEW YORK CITY

Dedicated to Judy, Joshua, and Shane.
And to Melinda, Michelle, and Jennifer, who
could all give Annie Oakley a run for her money.
"Ride until you drop."

A LEISURE BOOK®

May 2003

Published by

Dorchester Publishing Co., Inc.
276 Fifth Avenue
New York, NY 10001

ISBN 0-8439-3149-3

Visit us on the web at www.dorchesterpub.com.

Chapter One

Winter in the Rocky Mountains.

A white blanket of snow two feet deep covered the majestic peaks that reared thousands of feet into the crisp air. Ominous gray clouds drifted sluggishly from the northwest to the southeast, threatening to litter the primeval landscape with even more snow. High in the sky over one remote valley sailed a solitary eagle, sliding just below the clouds, its wings outspread as it gracefully soared on the uplifting currents.

In the valley, clustered near a narrow stream, browsed a small herd of mountain buffalo. Their shaggy coats insulated them from the sub-zero temperatures and their stringy beards were caked with snow and ice formed by their dripping saliva. Unlike their plains brethren, mountain buffalo stayed in the forested higher elevations the year round. They were as massive as their bovid kin, with males in their prime attaining a height of six feet at the shoulders, and weighing close to two thousand pounds. Their massive heads sported horns with a spread of three feet.

Many of the mighty beasts were using their powerful hoofs to clear snow from the underlying vegetation. Some simply stood and chewed their cuds. A young bull detached itself from the herd and moved a dozen yards to the treeline to the north. It selected a suitably stout tree and commenced rubbing its horns against the bark, doing so again and again until the bark began to wear away.

The breeze suddenly shifted, now coming from the north.

A second later the young bull stopped rubbing and loudly sniffed the air. It backed up several strides, tilting its huge head upward, its nostrils flaring.

Several others in the herd looked up and tested the breeze for scent. One of the animals abruptly bolted to the south, pounding through the stream to the opposite bank and throwing up a spray of snow as it ran toward the forest. In short order the rest did the same.

Spinning around, displaying remarkable agility for so enormous a beast, the young bull managed to take two strides before the sharp blast of a rifle shattered the stillness of the woodland. It dashed another three yards, then its front legs gave out and it crashed to the ground, rolling over and coming to rest on its right side.

The shot spurred the herd to greater speed. They gained the forest and plowed deep into the sheltering trees. In less than a minute the breaking of branches and the smashing of underbrush died down and only the whispering whistle of the wind remained. That, and the wheezing of the young bull.

A figure appeared to the north of the dying bison, a broad-shouldered, bearded man who advanced toward the brute with a Hawken rifle clenched firmly in his brawny hands. He wore a heavy red and black Mackinaw coat over beaded buckskins. Sturdy moccasins constructed from dressed elk skins protected his feet from the elements. A dark handcrafted hat fashioned from beaver pelts crowned his youthful head, scarcely containing his mane of long black hair.

In addition to the rifle he was armed with a pair of flintlock pistols which were positioned on both sides of the large silver buckle on the brown leather belt that encircled his Mackinaw at the waist. A butcher knife dangled from a beaded sheath on his left hip. Tucked under the belt and slanted over his left hip was a tomahawk. Crisscrossing his muscular chest were two indispensable items no mountaineer could do without—a powder-horn and a bullet-pouch.

Nineteen year old Nathaniel King stepped cautiously up to the young bull. His green eyes narrowed and his steely body tensed, ready for action should the beast suddenly rise. Buffalos were the most unpredictable critters on God's green earth, and when provoked they exhibited a fierce temperament that rivaled that of grizzly bears. They were tough, hardy animals, extremely difficult to kill. He'd heard of bison being shot over two-dozen times and still eluding the hapless hunters after them. Given the buffalos' reputation and disposition, he wasn't about to take reckless chances.

Nate stood over the brute and placed the Hawken barrel near its head. The bull still breathed, although laboriously, wheezing like a steam engine. Its eyes were wide. Blood flecked its mouth, dribbling from one corner, and the tip of its succulent tongue protruded. He pressed the rifle stock to his right shoulder and sighted on a point a few inches above the animal's left eye. Killing meat for the table was one thing; letting any creature suffer needlessly was another. His thumb pulled the hammer back until it clicked, then his trigger finger began to curl around the cool metal.

The bull then went into violent convulsions, lifting its head and snorting as its legs thrashed about wildly.

To avoid being gored Nate jumped back and waited for the fit to subside. In seconds the buffalo ceased moving entirely, its great head sagged onto the soft cushion of snow, and it expired with a protracted exhalation that stirred the settled flakes near its mouth.

Nate prodded the beast to make certain it was dead, then gazed skyward at the gray clouds. Soon it would snow, and unless he wanted to be caught in a blizzard he'd better hurry. Accordingly, he drew his keen edged butcher knife and set to work dressing the bull.

As he sliced open the abdominal cavity and warmed his hands in the beast's intestines, Nate thought about his beloved wife who eagerly awaited his return back at their cabin. He also thought of the new life taking form within her—the baby now five and a half months into the making in her womb.

He found it hard to accept that it was the middle of January. Only last April—April 1, 1828 to be exact—he'd left his father and mother, his job, his friends, and another woman he'd mistakenly believed he loved, back in New York City and ventured west to make his fortune. He'd given up his dreams of becoming an accountant in a prominent metropolitan firm to join his Uncle Zeke, the black sheep of the King family, who had gone into the wilderness many years before and never returned. Zeke had written to him, promising to share 'the greatest treasure in the world' if Nate would only join him beyond the frontier.

"What a fool I was!" Nate reflected, then immediately changed his mind. True, he'd envisioned becoming partners with Zeke in a lucrative fur trading enterprise, or perhaps in mining some of the fabulous veins of gold or silver rumored to exist in the Rockies. And true, Zeke's underlying intent had been to introduce Nate to the life of a *mountain man*, as some had taken to calling those rugged trappers and hunters who lived as the Indians did by eaking an existence from an invariably hostile land. The true treasure Zeke had wanted his nephew to possess was the gift of genuine freedom, of a life where a man's worth was measured by his character, strength, and endurance, and where the only constraints were those imposed by Nature and the will of the Almighty.

How ironic, Nate mused. If he hadn't entertained those foolish notions of attaining great wealth he never would have wound up enjoying that true freedom Zeke had prized above all else. And now he felt the same way! He'd grown to appreciate the value of the life his late uncle had extolled. He had grown to realize that God had never meant for humanity to be cooped up in filthy cities of stone and brick where men and women suffered through lives of quiet desperation.

Such a horrible existence was no longer for him!

He inhaled the frigid air and caught a whiff of the tangy scent of the bull's blood. *This* was the life. This was the way the Good Lord meant for men to live. He called no one master, had no obligations to anyone other than his wife and himself. There were no pompous politicians trying to dictate his behavior, no bosses looking over his shoulder.

In every sense of the word, he was a free man.

Nate chuckled, then paused in his busy work when a snowflake fell within an inch of his nose and landed on the ground near his knees. He stared upward and frowned, seeing many more such flakes descending. The snowfall had begun. Soon it would intensify to the point where he wouldn't be able to see his hands in front of his face.

He had a choice to make. Skinning and dressing the entire buffalo before the brunt of the storm hit would be impossible. Either he made a lean-to in the trees and waited for the snow to stop, which could take hours, or he removed enough meat to feed Winona and himself for a week or so and returned home. He'd wandered less than two miles from the cabin since he began hunting, so the latter prospect was infinitely more appealing.

Nate hurriedly removed a sizeable strip of hide and carved off a thigh section of meat. He placed them to one side, then went about gathering limbs with which to cover the bull. Concealing it wouldn't do much good where wolves or panthers were concerned, since both could smell fresh blood half a mile off if the wind was right. But the neatly arranged limbs might prevent the kill from being spotted by other animals or by Indians who might be in the area.

The snow was falling steadily by the time Nate finished and wrapped the meat in the hide. He straightened, grabbed his Hawken, and headed to the northeast. The nearest peaks were obscured by the gradually building storm, depriving him of the landmarks he ordinarily relied on to guide his steps. Consequently, he moved slower than he normally would, selecting his route with care to avoid blundering into a ravine or over a cliff.

He made relatively good progress for the first twenty minutes or so. Then the rate of falling snow dramatically increased and he could barely distinguish trees twenty feet ahead.

The Hawken in his right hand, the bundle of meat under his left arm, Nate trudged onward, determined to get through no matter what. Several more minutes elapsed.

He felt something moist drip onto his left hand, first one drop, then others, and looking down he discovered that blood had seeped through the hide and onto his forearm. He'd removed the deerskin gloves Winona had sewn for him at the onset of cold weather in order to shoot at the bull, and he now paused to take them from the pockets of his Mackinaw and gratefully eased his chilled fingers into the soft material.

Taking the rifle and bundle again in hand, Nate resumed hiking through the sea of white and traveled a hundred yards before he heard the first of the howls. He halted, listening to the distant wail, wondering if the sound might be the wind. A second howl, slightly closer, dispelled his wishful thinking.

There were wolves abroad.

He hastened off. Normally wolves posed no problems for solitary humans. The stealthy and wily carnivores would run at the sight of man. There were exceptions to the rule, however. If a single wolf or a pack had gone long without food, they would tempt fate. And in the winter, when game was scarce and bringing prey such as deer and elk down became extremely difficult even for skilled stalkers, the wolves would hunt anything that moved.

Nate had heard a story once about a trapper who lost a leg to a pack of ravenous wolves and he had no intention of suffering a similar or worse fortune. He forged diligently northeastward until he ascended a rise located less than a mile from the lake near which his cabin stood.

At that moment more howls erupted to his rear and they were much, much closer.

Hefting the Hawken, Nate increased his pace. The wolves were on his trail. They must be following the scent of the dripping blood. He considered abandoning the meat, of simply leaving the bundle for them to find and buying the time he would need to make his escape, but the thought of Winona going hungry firmed his resolve. His wife needed the food. She was eating for two and she depended on him to provide the nourishment she required. He wasn't about to let her down.

The slope was slick and Nate nearly lost his footing several times en route to the bottom. He estimated he had another thirty feet to go when a strident howl, sounding as if it were at the top of the rise, caused him to glance over his shoulder in alarm. The snow screened the crest from his view. He derived some small comfort from the fact that since he couldn't see the wolves, they couldn't see him. Or so he hoped.

As Nate faced front his left foot hit a slippery spot and swept out from under him. He frantically tried to regain his balance, to no avail. Gravity brought him down onto his backside and he started to slide, gathering momentum with every yard. A small boulder loomed in his path and he threw himself to the left, hoping to roll out of harm's way. He wasn't completely successful.

A searing pain lanced his right leg as his shin struck the boulder with a jarring impact. Nate grit his teeth to keep from crying out. He spun, out of control, and tumbled the rest of the distance to the bottom, landing hard on his shoulders in a mound of snow.

Dazed, Nate struggled into a sitting position and took stock. He'd instinctively retained his grip on the rifle and the meat. Grunting, he tried to rise, his right leg in torment. From his rear came a low growl and he twisted to behold several dark four-legged forms gliding down the slope.

The wolves had found him.

Chapter Two

His pulse quickening, Nate surged to his feet and swung around to face the onrushing shadows. All three timber wolves halted, the nearest approximately fifteen feet off, their features shrouded by the driving snow. He could distinguish the general outline of their sleek bodies, but nothing more.

One of the beasts snarled.

Nate waited expectantly, his every nerve tingling, for the wolves to charge. He didn't dare fire while holding the buffalo meat. Shooting a powerful Hawken accurately one-handed was next to impossible and might well result in a busted limb. But he wasn't about to let go of the meat except as a last resort since he knew full well the wolves would be on it in a flash.

A minute went by. Two minutes. And still the

wolves only stood there, silently regarding him, perhaps taking his measure in their bestial way.

What now? Nate asked himself. The longer he stayed put, the colder he'd become. His reflexes would be dulled, even sluggish. The wolves would have a distinct advantage. He couldn't allow that to happen.

Taking a deep breath, Nate slowly backed away from the animals, ignoring the acute discomfort in his right leg. His eyes darted from wolf to wolf in anticipation of being attacked but the threesome were as still as statues. After going a dozen feet he warily wheeled and resumed his trek.

The storm intensified again, the falling snow becoming a virtual swirling white wall, obliterating the landscape in all directions. Nate lost sight of the wolves, and he paused to listen for their footfalls, but heard only the swishing snow and gusting wind. Lowering his head into the flake laden air, he made for home, vowing not to stop again until he held Winona in his arms.

Repeatedly Nate bumped into obstacles; logs, trees, rocks, and boulders were impossible to see. His right leg pained him less with every step, leading him to believe it was only badly bruised or sprained but not broken.

If the wolves were out there, they made no sound. Once, briefly, a shadowy form materialized on the right, then just as promptly vanished.

Nate couldn't find any points of reference and had no idea where he was. He guessed he was moving in the right direction and stubbornly forged onward, not daunted in the least at the prospect of being lost. There were trees all around him and it would be an easy task to construct a temporary shelter that would keep him relatively comfortable and safe until the snow abated.

Knowing he must only have three-quarters of a

mile to cover inspired him with hope that he would find the cabin before too long. Granted, spying a lone structure in the midst of a raging snowstorm wouldn't be easy, but he should be able to locate the lake without too much difficulty, and once he did finding the cabin would be a simple task.

Nate trudged through the forest for an indefinite period, losing all track of time. His exertion made him sweat, and the sweat in turn cooled and caused him to shiver. Oh, what he wouldn't give for a roaring fire and a hot cup of coffee!

He skirted a huge pine tree blocking his path and stopped to rest for a moment. The instant he did, something plowed into his legs from the rear and bowled him over. Caught off-guard, he felt teeth tear into his left calf as he fell onto his back. And then whatever had attacked him was gone, evaporating like a specter into the mist of white particles.

The wolves!

Nate rolled onto his right elbow and shoved upright. A scan of the area showed only snow. He bent down to look at his calf and found blood staining his legging and moccasin.

What were they up to? Why nip at him and run?

He hastened into the storm, hoping he wouldn't lose too much blood. If so, he might as well dig a hole in the ground and bury himself because he'd never reach the cabin alive.

Another streaking figure hurtled out of the snow and struck him in the lower legs.

Again Nate went down and was bitten, only this time on the opposite leg. The wolf disappeared into the storm. He swiftly rose, his other leg bleeding, and tried in vain to spot the beasts.

Somewhere to his rear one of the predators howled.

Nate turned and ran blindly, seeking to elude them and not paying much attention to the terrain. When a pine loomed in front of him he slowed, then dropped to his knees and scooted under its overhanging branches. He placed his back to the trunk, deposited the meat at his side, and gripped the rifle in both hands.

Now let them come!

Their tactics abruptly made complete sense. He'd once witnessed a pack of seven wolves kill a young moose by continually harassing it—taking turns running in and biting its flanks until eventually the moose collapsed and was easy prey for their raking teeth. These crafty wolves were trying the same devious ploy on him.

Thanks to the long tree limbs Nate could see for a few yards in all directions. The wolves wouldn't be able to get at him without being spotted. He cocked the Hawken and impatiently awaited the next assault.

His mind strayed to thoughts of Winona. He imagined her sitting by the fireplace in their cabin, probably worried half to death about him. Just so she stayed in there and didn't come looking for him.

What was that?

Something moved in the snow, a fleeting flicker that gave no hint of its cause.

The wolves had him boxed in. If he could only slay one of them the rest might leave. But how to accomplish the deed? He pondered the problem until an idea occured to him that brought a grin to his lips.

Taking the bundle of meat, he slid it out until the hide sat just at the edge of the sheltering tree limbs. Then he put his back to the trunk and trained the rifle barrel on the bait. The range was only eight feet. If he stayed alert, he couldn't miss.

Although the wolves had to know the buffalo meat was there, they made no attempt to claim it for their own.

Nate wondered if the animals were trying to wait

him out. Sooner or later he'd grow drowsy, perhaps doze off. Stealing the bundle would then be child's play. He reminded himself not to underestimate the intelligence of the three creatures.

Sure enough, lethargy set in and his eyelids fluttered and drooped. He forced himself awake and examined his wounds. Both were bleeding profusely, which must be weakening him considerably.

Nate shook his head and went to yawn. A vague shadow popped into sight near the buffalo meat and he froze, his finger touching the trigger.

Ever so cautiously the wolf came forward.

He could see its head now, its mouth curved back in a feral snarl and a hungry gleam in its eyes. The wolf was lean, nearly gaunt, and had long been without food. Under different circumstances he might have been moved to pity the animal, but his wife's need took precedence over the wolf's.

Nate sighted along the barrel, fixing a bead on the beast's sloping forehead. He resisted the temptation to fire until the wolf stood right beside the bundle, about to bite into the hide, and then he squeezed the trigger.

The sharp retort was amplified by the limbs overhead. At the sound the wolf sprang backwards, or tried to, but got only a foot before crumbling in the snow, a neat hole smack dab between its eyes.

Nate lost no time. He hastily reloaded, placing the rifle butt on the ground and pouring sufficient black powder from his powder-horn into the palm of his left hand. He fed the grains down the muzzle, wrapped a ball in a patch, then used the ramrod to shove the ball down on top of the powder. Replacing the ramrod under the barrel, he scoured the vicinity for the remaining wolves.

Given the well known fact that wolves, like most animals in the Rockies, were notoriously gun shy,

Nate concluded that the pair had fled. A nagging doubt, however, rooted him in place for five minutes. Finally he moved to the dead wolf, debating whether to take its skin, and decided his first priority was to reach Winona.

Clasping the bundle under his left arm, Nate slid out from under the pine tree and tramped into the storm. Both legs were stiff and sore. After walking a bit they loosened up but hurt terribly. His eagerness to reach the cabin mounted with each stride he took.

So intent was he on finding his home, he failed to watch his back trail, so the first inkling he had of impending danger was the throaty growl of a charging wolf to his rear. Whirling, he dropped the meat and attempted to level the Hawken, but the barrel was still slanted toward the ground when the two wolves hurtled through the air and slammed into his chest.

Nate was knocked down hard onto his shoulders with a pair of snapping jaws within inches of his face. He released the Hawken and grabbed a hairy throat in each hand, digging his fingers into their flesh, striving to hold them at bay.

The wolves were in a primal fury. They clawed at his coat and bit at his head, their combined weight and strength formidable.

It was all Nate could do to hold on. One of the wolves snared the tip of his chin, its tapered teeth digging in deep. In dread of having one of them bite into his neck, Nate frantically threw himself to the right and heaved, then tried to regain his footing.

Both wolves recovered instantaneously and scrambled to their feet. The larger of the duo sprang.

In a virtual blur Nate drew his right flintlock and snapped off a shot, the tip of the pistol barrel almost touching the wolf's nose when it discharged a small cloud of smoke and lethal lead. The ball bored into the animal's skull, the impact flipping it onto its back. The last wolf never even paused. Growling, the beast leaped and chomped down on the extended arm.

Nate almost screamed from the agony. The flintlock fell from his grasp and he arched his spine, then dropped his left hand to the butcher knife. His fingers closed around the hilt and he swept the razor-edged blade up and in, sinking it into the wolf's exposed chest.

Snarling savagely, the wolf opened its jaws, darted to the left, and closed in again.

Swinging the butcher knife in an arc, Nate cut a furrow in the wolf's face, nearly taking out an eye. The beast bounded out of his reach and crouched, its teeth exposed. He lunged, swinging recklessly, and drove the animal farther back.

For a moment the two adversaries eyed one another.

Then the wolf came in fast and low, going for the legs.

Nate twisted to the left and speared the knife at the wolf's back. He scored, slicing its fur open. In a twinkling the animal pivoted and pounced, burying its teeth into his left leg.

The *pain*! Never had Nate known such excrutiating torture. He cried out, dropping the knife, and endeavored to jerk his leg lose. The wolf held firm, however, and in desperation he drew his other flintlock, pressed the barrel to the top of the animal's cranium, cocked the hammer, and fired.

Its body going limp, the wolf collapsed on the spot, blood and bits of gray matter spurting from the hole in its head. But even in death the beast's jaws stayed locked on Nate's leg.

Squatting, Nate stuck the flintlock under his belt and gripped the wolf's jaws, trying to pry them apart. He strained for all he was worth, his face becoming red, his veins bulging. With a supreme effort he managed to wrench the teeth from his flesh and sank back on the snow, exhausted.

But Nate realized this ordeal was far from over. He grit his teeth and sat up to inspect his wounds. The amount of blood he was losing appalled him. He couldn't waste precious time in recuperating. He had to get on his feet and get to the cabin or he would surely die.

Spurred by the realization of his own mortality, Nate collected his weapons, tucked the prized meat under his left arm, and hastened in what he hoped was the direction of the cabin and the lake. He felt blood trickling down his arm and legs and tried not to dwell on it. Keep going, he prodded himself. Just keep going. You'll reach the cabin.

Countless snow flakes swirled around him and caked his hat, coat, and moccasins. He trudged ever forward, his shoulders hunched, shivering more and more as time wore on. His legs became progressively weaker. He bumped into objects, recovered his balance, and pressed on.

I'm coming, Winona! he wanted to shout.

Nate's senses swam. He had no idea how far he traveled or how much time had elapsed. It took all of his concentration merely to move one foot ahead of the other. Left. Right. Left. Right. With single-minded purpose he plowed toward the woman he loved.

I'm coming, Winona!

Numbness set in, creeping up his legs to his thighs, an odd tingling compounded by his now constant shivering. He wished he could lie down and rest. A few hours sleep might restore his vitality.

What was he thinking? Nate chided himself for his momentary weakness and walked on. His vision blurred and he was startled when he smacked into a tree and fell to his knees. Grimacing, he willed his legs to straighten so he could continue but they refused to obey his mental command. He tried again with the same result.

This couldn't be happening.

He couldn't die now, not when he'd found the greatest happiness any man had ever known.

Nate swallowed and felt nauseous. He tried a third time to stand. Instead, a strange wave of black emptiness engulfed his consciousness and he began to pitch onto his face. In that final second before the void claimed him, he raised his head and called out the name of the woman who meant more to him than life itself, shouting at the top of his lungs in defiance to the wilderness that had bested him: "WWWIIINNNOOONNNAAA!"

Then he struck the ground. The last sensation he experienced was the soft snow against his skin.

Chapter Three

He seemed to be at the bottom of a murky pool. Far above him lay the shimmering surface. He pushed off from the bottom and swam with even, strong strokes toward the beckoning light. Oddly, for every stroke he took the surface receded the same distance. He made no headway. His lungs began to ache.

With a start he realized that he wasn't in a pool. Water didn't envelope him; a heavy, moist air did, a palpable substance unlike any he'd ever known or heard about. He stroked harder, kicking his legs but still he made no progress. His lungs began to ache.

Somewhere someone shouted, a muffled cry he barely heard. He flailed his arms and pumped his legs with all his might, yet the surface mocked him by receding farther. Something materialized above him, a huge mass that swept down toward him and blocked out the light. He opened his mouth to scream and felt his wind cut off.

"Nate! Nate! It's me!"

The urgent voice, so intimately familiar, penetrated to the core of his being, stirring his very soul, and Nate became instantly wide awake. His eyes snapped open and he looked around him in confusion, fearing he'd dreamed hearing her. "Winona?" he blurted, then saw her seated beside him on the right. They were both on the bed in their cabin.

"I am here, husband," his wife stated, using her native tongue, the musical language of the Shoshone tribe.

"Thank the Lord," Nate breathed in English, his eyes drinking in her beauty. He knew she would understand him. They each spoke the other's language with a fair degree of fluency, although he would be the first to admit that she spoke more English than he did Shoshone. Frequently they conducted conversations in both tongues, as much to keep in practice as anything else.

Like most women in her tribe, Winona possessed high, prominent cheekbones that served to accent her natural loveliness. Hip-length, luxurious black hair and lively brown eyes imbued her with an aura of innate vitality. A beaded buckskin dress, bulging at the abdomen, covered her otherwise supple figure.

"The Great Mystery was indeed watching over you," Winona said softly, reaching over to tenderly stroke his brow. "If I hadn't heard you yell, you would have died in the blizzard."

The blizzard! Nate's memory of shooting the young bull and the attack by the wolves returned in a rush and he went to sit up. Searing pain in his right arm made him wince and look down at himself. All he had on were his leggins and they had been slit from their bottom edges to his thighs to afford access to his wounds.

"Please stay still," Winona urged. "The wolves you fought tore you very badly and you're weak. I put herbs on the bites to help them heal."

"Thank you," Nate said gratefully. He frowned as he studied the ragged gashes in his body; there were two on his left leg, one on his right, a nasty laceration on his right arm several inches above the wrist, and the injury to his chin. Small wonder he ached from his head to his toes. "How did you know it was wolves?"

"You talked in your sleep," Winona said.

Nate looked at the window, at the narrow space between the sill and the flap, and saw snow still falling outside. From the amount of subdued light it must be daytime. "How long was I unconscious?"

"Most of yesterday and all night. It's morning now."

"What?" Nate said in surprise. To him it was as if mere minutes had elapsed. He keenly appreciated owing his life to her. Had she not found him, he'd be in the spirit world, as the Indians liked to say. "You heard me call your name?"

Winona nodded. "You were only twenty steps from the rear of the cabin when you collapsed."

"And you carried me inside by yourself?" Nate asked in alarm.

"No," Winona said, and grinned. "A black bear helped me."

"This is no joking matter," Nate said. "You shouldn't be lifting something as heavy as I am in your condition." He touched her bulging belly. "You took a great risk."

"Don't be silly. I couldn't leave you there to die."

Nate gazed affectionately into her eyes. "I'm sorry for the trouble I caused you."

"Yes, you were a lot of trouble," Winona stated in mock seriousness. "I can't wait to tell my people how the mighty Grizzly Killer let himself be beaten by a few hungry wolves."

Her cheery laughter a second later prompted him to join in. He could readily imagine the mirth her story would provoke in the Shoshones, who possessed a keen sense of humor.

The mighty Grizzly Killer! Nate recalled the Cheyenne Warrior called White Eagle who had bestowed the name on him months ago after he'd tangled with his first brown bear, as some of the mountaineers referred to that most savage denizen of the Rockies. Somehow, the title had stuck. Perhaps the fact he'd been compelled to slay three of the fierce brutes since leaving the States had something to do with it, for now the Cheyennes, the Shoshones, the dreaded Blackfeet, the Bannocks, Utes, Nez Perces, and Flatheads all knew him by his Indian name.

To Nate's amazement, tales of his presumed exploits were being told around many a campfire from the Mississippi to the mountains. He could partially understand being a topic of conversation for the trappers, who spent every evening enjoying fireside chats about the latest news and gossip. But he'd been stunned to learn that word of his exploits had passed among the various Indian tribes gathered for the rendezvous last year at Bear Lake, or Sweet Lake as some called it.

Winona herself had told him that her people were boasting to all who would listen of their friendship with the famous Grizzly Killer. The white man who could kill a Grizzly with a mere knife, the free trapper who had saved their tribe from the Blackfeet had married one of their prettiest maidens.

Nate often found his spreading notoriety embarrassing. If he wasn't careful, he'd soon be nearly as famous as Jed Smith, Jim Bridger, or Joseph Walker.

Or Shakespeare McNair.

Thinking of the wise old mountain man who had been his mentor after the death of his Uncle Zeke, Nate smiled and wished Shakespeare was still staying at the cabin. He missed his friend's companionship, missed Shakespeare's wit and insights. If he lived only half as long and acquired only half as much wisdom as McNair, he'd be two times as smart as the average person.

"Would you care for some buffalo stew, husband?" Winona inquired.

Nate stared at the corner of the cabin where the pots and pans were kept, then at the stone fireplace he'd built shortly before winter set in. A heavy pot purchased at the rendezvous hung over low flames. "You brought in the bundle I was carrying too?"

"I couldn't pry your fingers off it," Winona revealed. "And after all the trouble you went to in bringing the meat back, I had no intention of leaving it to rot."

The prospect of food caused Nate's stomach to growl loudly. "Yes, I'd like some stew very much. Even better, I could eat a thick, juicy steak."

"You've been without food for too long to eat steak now," Winona cautioned him. "A few days of soup and herbs will restore your strength. Then you can have steak."

Nate pretended to pout. "I had no idea wives could be so much like mothers."

Rising, Winona placed a hand on her stomach. "Motherhood comes naturally to women." She stepped around the end of the bed and walked toward the fireplace.

Settling back, Nate fondly watched her stir the contents of the pot. Despite his wounds and the attendant pain, he was supremely content. Simply being alive made him thankful. Having the most wonderful wife on the North American continent was an added gift. To think, if he'd stayed back in New York he might have wound up married to Adeline!

Adeline Van Buren was the exquisitely cultured— some would say exquisitely *spoiled*—daughter of an extremely wealthy man in New York City. Because Nate's father had known her father, they'd become acquainted. Her charm and radiant good looks had mesmerized Nate and he'd fallen head over heels for her. To his utter astonishment, Adeline had reciprocated. They'd even discussed marriage. Acutely aware of his financial shortcomings, Nate had eagerly jumped at the chance to share in his uncle's wealth in an effort to provide Adeline with the many luxuries to which she'd grown accustomed.

How strange fate could be, Nate reflected. He'd left New York with every intention of returning to Adeline a rich man. Now he didn't care if he ever went East or saw her again, although infrequently a twinge of guilt bothered him. One day, maybe, he would take a trip back and explain everything to her. He owed her that much, at least.

"I dried and salted most of the meat," Winona announced, interrupting his contemplation. "We have enough to last until the new moon."

"The cold should preserve the rest of the kill," Nate mentioned. "In two or three days I'll go get more."

"You will not go anywhere until you are healed."

Nate chuckled. "I thought Indian wives always go along with whatever their husbands want."

A spontaneous laugh erupted from Winona's lips. "Where did you ever hear such a crazy thing?"

"Here and there."

"Indian women are taught to always obey their husbands, yes. But we also speak our minds when the need arises. If our husbands behave like idiots, we tell them so," Winona said, and smirked. "Although not in public."

Nate thought of all the newspaper stories he'd read about Indians back in New York and frowned. Most had contained dreadful inaccuracies and exaggerations. Many editorialists had claimed that all Indians were savages who deserved to be forced off their lands to make room for the whites. And no less a personage than Andrew Jackson, the hero of the Battle of New Orleans who was running for President of the United States, had gone so far as to state the Indians were an inferior race.

The fools. What did they know about Indians, about Indian values and the Indian way of life? Nate would like to line up every one of the bigots and personally put a ball between their eyes. He wondered if Jackson had won the election and reminded himself to ask the next trappers he encountered. If so, it did not bode well for Indians everywhere.

"Nate?"

He looked up to find her regarding him solemnly. "Yes?"

"May I ask you a question?"

"Since when does an Indian woman need her husband's permission to ask a question?" Nate quipped.

"Do you ever regret marrying me?"

Shocked, Nate forgot himself and rose onto his elbows. "Why do you ask?"

"Do you?"

"Of course not. I love you with all my heart."

"But would you be happier married to a white woman?"

Nate's brow knit as he tried to ascertain the reason for her concern. He'd never mentioned a word to her about Adeline. "No, I wouldn't," he stated firmly. "I couldn't possibly be happier than I am right at this moment. I'm insulted, Winona, that you would even think to ask."

"I don't mean to offend you."

"Then why bring it up?"

Winona stopped stirring and faced him. "Who is Adeline?"

If the roof had collapsed onto his head, Nate wouldn't have been more flabbergasted than he was. "Where did you hear her name?"

"From you. While you were unconscious."

Nate detected hurt in her eyes and struggled to keep his voice calm, his face composed. "What did I say about her?"

"Nothing. You only called her name. Four times."

"I see," Nate said, stalling, debating whether to reveal the whole truth. He didn't want to upset Winona more than she already had been. "Adeline Van Buren is a woman I knew in New York City. We were friends."

"Only friends?"

"More than friends," Nate admitted. "We were thinking about getting married."

"Oh," Winona said, the word barely audible. She turned to the pot again.

"Come here," Nate said.

Winona didn't budge.

"Please."

Her slender shoulders slumping, Winona let go of the ladle and came over to the edge of the bed.

"Sit down. Please."

Winona complied reluctantly, averting her gaze.

Grunting, Nate sat up and placed his hands on her shoulders. "Look at me."

She did so, moisture rimming her eyes.

"You're all upset for no reason," Nate assured her. "Adeline Van Buren means nothing to me. I have no regrets over leaving her." He paused, pulled Winona forward, and gently kissed her. "I married you, dearest, because I love you more than any woman

I've ever known. More than I could ever care for Adeline. I want to spend the rest of my life with you, raising a family and growing old together. And, God willing, I want to be buried at your side when we both go to meet our Maker." He paused again. "Do you understand? I would *not* be happier married to a white woman. I would be miserable without you."

Winona suddenly threw her arms around him and pressed her face to his neck. "Thank you, husband," she said quietly.

Nate felt her tears on his skin and a lump formed in his throat. He stroked her hair, chiding himself for not telling her about Adeline sooner. Causing her misery was the last thing he ever wanted to do. He opened his mouth to tell her as much when from outside the cabin came a sound that inevitably heralded trouble.

The crack of a shot.

Chapter Four

Nate let his arms drop and Winona promptly stood, their mutual anxiety forgotten.

Nate put his palms on the bed and swung his legs over the side.

"What do you think you are doing?"

Nate ignored the question, touched his soles to the rough wooden floor, and shoved. He succeeded in rising although his legs shrieked in protest. Swaying precariously, he might have fallen had not Winona quickly stepped to his side and looped an arm around his waist.

"You should stay in bed," she scolded him.

"Help me to the window," Nate said, and moved stiffly when she reluctantly complied. They stood next to the deerskin flap that his Uncle Zeke had tacked to the top of the window years ago when the cabin was built. Winona had rolled up the bottom

edge half an inch and tied it at that height for
ventilation. "How far off do you think that shot was?"

"The other side of the lake."

Nate nodded. "I'd guess the same." He bent at the
waist and peered out the crack. All he saw was snow
and more snow. "Who would be out in weather like
this?" he asked absently.

"Utes."

Incipient apprehension flared in Nate's breast. He
was in no condition to do battle with a band of
bloodthirsty Utes. The cabin was located in their
territory and his uncle had fought off marauding
warriors on several occasions. "I hope you're
wrong," he said.

"Even if there is a war party in the area, I doubt
they can find our cabin."

Nate liked the way she referred to their home as
"our." He listened for a minute, then began to
straighten.

From the distance came a second shot, muffled by
the heavy snow and echoing off the high peaks that
rimmed the valley in which the cabin was situated.

"That one was a little closer," Nate commented, at
a loss to explain the gunfire. Certainly no one would
be hunting in such inclement weather; seeing the
game would be impossible. Perhaps the shots were
signals of some sort.

"You should lie down," Winona proposed. "I will
keep watch out the window."

"That's my job," Nate disagreed. "Get me a chair
and I'll be fine."

Hesitating, Winona frowned to emphasize her dis-
pleasure, then went to a nearby chair he'd constructed with his own hands and set it in front of the
sill. "Here."

"Thank you," Nate said gratefully, sinking down.
He didn't know how much longer he could have

stayed on his feet. Uncharacteristic weakness pervaded him and he longed to curl up on the bed and sleep for a week.

"Would you like your stew?"

"Yes. And my guns and my other set of buckskins."

Winona wisely brought the Hawken and both flintlocks over first. None were loaded. He frowned at his oversight. No matter how badly he'd been hurt, reloading should have been his first priority. Nate requested the powder-horn and the ammunition-pouch and prepared all three guns in case there should be uninvited visitors. Next he put on the clothes, wedged the pistols under his belt, then started in on the stew. Never had buffalo meat and broth tasted so delicious. He chewed each morsel and savored every drop.

Carting over the other chair, Winona took a seat on his left and watched him finish off the meal. "Would you like more?"

"Not now," Nate said, rubbing his stomach. "Another drop and I'll be too drowsy to stay awake." He gave her the bowl and positioned the Hawken on his lap. The meal had invigorated him and he felt ready to wrestle a bear. A *small* bear. He was close enough to the window that a slight, cool breeze touched his face and made him feel chilly, a convincing reminder he mustn't push himself too hard or he'd be back in bed in no time.

Winona moved off, and when next she stepped into view she had a heavy buffalo robe draped over her shoulders. She walked to the front door and gripped the wooden latch.

"Where are you heading?" Nate inquired.

"One of us must check on the horses."

"I'll do it," Nate said, rising.

"Please, husband. You must stay inside and stay warm. I will be back soon."

Nate stood. Their four animals were in a pen he'd constructed on the south side of the cabin. Verifying the horses were all right would take only a minute, but he didn't like the notion of Winona venturing out in the blizzard when there might be Utes in the vicinity. "I'll go."

"You're being stubborn. I will be fine."

Moving over to where his patched Mackinaw hung on a hook on the wall, Nate propped the rifle against his left leg, took the red coat down, and slipped his arms into the sleeves. "Thank you for sewing the rips."

"Don't change the subject," Winona said stiffly. "You shouldn't go out and you know it."

"If it will make you feel any better," Nate offered to appease her, "why don't we both go?"

"If you insist. But stay close to me."

Nate found his moccasins, put them on, and retrieved the Hawken. "I'll go first," he offered.

A blast of icy wind tore into their cozy home the moment he opened the stout door. Tucking his chin to his chest, Nate steeled himself and walked outside. The whipping snow obscured everything beyond a range of fifteen feet. Moist flakes lashed his cheeks.

Winona closed the door behind them.

To their left, stacked against the cabin, was the immense stack of firewood Nate had cut for the winter. Since their home faced due east, he turned right, staying close to the wall as he walked to the corner and peered around the edge. The snow prevented him from seeing the entire pen. He reasoned that the animals would instinctively congregate at the west side of the fence where the forest beyond was thickest and would act as a windbreak.

Nate walked to the pen and began to follow the fence around. He glanced at his wife, who was to his left, and smiled. She gave him a stare every bit as frosty as the blizzard. Annoyed that she didn't appreciate his selfless gesture in not wanting to expose her to potential danger, he trudged around the south end of the pen and halted when he finally spied the four horses.

The animals had indeed gathered to the west and were huddled together. They gazed at him longingly, as if in the expectation he would make them warm again.

Winona stepped to a pile of grass they had collected to use as feed and dumped several arm loads over the top rail, in reality a long limb like all the rest Nate had employed to fashion the fence.

None of the horses moved.

Taking his wife's elbow, Nate started to retrace their route. The cold was causing him to shiver and he was eager to get inside where the fire would warm him. He entertained the idea of eating another bowl of stew, and thus preoccupied he hiked to within a yard of the entrance when he stopped in midstride.

The front door hung open.

Stunned, Nate exchanged an alarmed glance with Winona. He leveled the Hawkin and eased cautiously to the jamb. Had someone been watching the cabin and seen them depart? He rejected that idea because of the limited field of visibility, but then a shadow flitted across the doorway.

Any doubt that there was someone inside evaporated and Nate's features hardened. It must be Utes, he deduced. If so, they'd pay dearly for violating his home. He cocked the hammer, being careful not to let it click loudly, and peeked into the cabin. His anger gave way to baffled amusement.

A portly white man attired in buckskins stood at the fireplace ladling stew into his fleshy mouth as swiftly as he could dip the implement. He sported a scruffy beard and a thin moustache. On his head perched a cap made from an otter skin. A Kentucky rifle leaned against the wall nearby.

Nate slid into the room and advanced halfway to the fireplace before speaking. "That's my stew you're helping yourself to, stranger."

At the sound of Nate's voice the man started, dropped the ladle, and spun, some of the broth dripping down over his fat jowls. He blinked a few times, then glanced at the Kentucky rifle.

"You'll be dead before you touch it," Nate warned gravely.

The man looked past him as Winona entered, then swallowed and licked his lips.

"Do you have a name?" Nate asked.

"Kennedy, sir," the man responded in a high, whining voice. "Isaac Kennedy at your service."

"And what are you doing helping yourself to our stew?"

"I'm sorry," Kennedy said, and went on in a rush of words as if anxious to explain before he was shot. "I truly am. But I was cold and starving and when I stumbled on your cabin and no one answered my knock I just opened the door and saw the stew and couldn't resist the temptation."

Unable to suppress a grin, Nate let the Hawken barrel droop. He shifted and glanced at Winona, then nodded at the door. She scanned the area outside before closing it.

"I didn't mean no harm, sir," Kennedy said. "But I was so hungry. I haven't eaten for over twenty-four hours."

"That long, eh?" Nate responded with a straight face. He studied the stranger, trying to ascertain the man's character. One fact was obvious; Isaac Kennedy had no place being in the wilderness. The man clearly was no mountaineer.

"And it's so cold out there," Kennedy said, shuddering. "I swear I nearly froze to death a dozen times."

Nate had a thought. "Was that you doing the shooting earlier?"

"No, sir. That must have been my two partners," Kennedy said. "We became separated and they were probably searching for me. I heard them shoot but I couldn't answer them."

"Why not?"

"I snagged my powder-horn on a tree limb and it was torn off. I tried to find it, but couldn't."

Nate stared at the Kentucky rifle. "Your gun isn't loaded?"

"No, sir. I forgot to load it after I shot at a rabbit the day before yesterday."

"It's not very smart to wander around the mountains with an empty rifle."

"I know. Newton and Lambert are always reminding me to reload right after I fire, but I keep forgetting."

"I take it that Newton and Lambert are your partners?"

"Yes, sir."

"Stop calling me sir. My name is Nate King," Nate revealed, and motioned at Winona. "This is Winona, my wife."

"Pleased to make your acquaintance," Kennedy said, wiping his left sleeve across his chin. He looked at the Hawken and gulped. "You're not fixing to shoot me, are you?"

"No," Nate said. He gave the rifle to Winona, who hung it on a rack on the north wall next to the bed. Removing the Mackinaw, he exposed the two flint-locks and saw the man's eyes widen. "What are you and your partners doing in this neck of the woods?" he asked as he hung the coat up.

"We're trappers, sir."

"Is that a fact?" Nate remarked, concealing his disbelief. Why the man should lie, he didn't know. But if Isaac Kennedy was a trapper, then Nate was the Queen of England. "I'm a free trapper myself. Do you work for one of the fur companies?"

"No," Kennedy answered quickly, a bit too quickly. "We're free trappers also."

"Have you been at it long?"

"Newton and Lambert have. This is my first trip into the Rockies."

"I never would have guessed," Nate said. He gestured at one of the chairs. "Why don't you take a seat, Isaac, and we'll give you a bowl of stew."

"I don't want to impose."

"Nonsense. We wouldn't be good Samaritans if we didn't feed those in need."

Rubbing his thick hands together in anticipation, Kennedy grinned and walked over to sit down. "Thank you. I'll never forget your hospitality. I can't get over how friendly folks are west of the Mississippi. The people in Independence, Missouri, were courteous and helpful to a fault."

Nate idly scratched the left side of his beard, carefully avoiding the bite mark. Independence, located on the very edge of the frontier, had been founded two years ago and served as the start-off point for many traveling into these vast uncharted lands. "I gather you're from the East."

"Ohio," Kennedy answered, watching as Winona moved to the pot with a bowl in her hand.

"Did you come all this way on foot?"

"No sir. My horse ran away when I fell off it."

Nate wasn't certain he'd heard correctly. "You fell off your horse?"

"Right after I snagged my ammo-pouch on that tree," Kennedy said, unable to take his eyes off the stew being ladled into the bowl.

"Tell me, Isaac. What did you do before you decided to become a trapper?"

"I was a merchant. Owned my own store," Kennedy said, almost drooling as Winona approached him with the steaming stew.

"And where do you and your partners plan to do your trapping?"

Kennedy gazed at Nate and replied in all innocence: "In Ute country."

Chapter Five

The tall man stood beside his horse in the sheltering midst of a stand of high pines and peered skyward at the diminishing snowfall. He patted his mount, then swung lithely into the saddle. Buckskins and a brown wool coat covered his thin frame. His angular face was surrounded by a black beard at the bottom and a tangled mop of dark hair at the top. Eyes the color of a high country lake but colder than the snow regarded his surroundings with the alert air of a seasoned mountaineer. A perpetual sneer curled his thin lips. In his right hand he clutched a rifle. Snug under the black belt girding his coat was a flintlock.

He goaded his horse out of the pines and across a tract of clear land toward a jumble of boulders at the base of the mountains bordering the valley on the east side. His body swayed slightly with the stride of his animal, as if the horse and him were one entity.

As he neared the boulders he surveyed the area until he saw a spiral of smoke rising from behind several monoliths positioned close together. Urging his horse to go faster he soon arrived at the site and passed between a pair of boulders each the size of a house to find a campfire blazing and another man squatting by the flames who looked up at his advent on the scene.

The second man also wore buckskins and a black coat. He possessed a stockier build and wore a cap constructed from a wolf pelt with the tail dangling down his back. His hair was brown, as were his eyes. A short, trimmed beard lent his face a squarish profile. Leaning on a rock near his left hand was a modified .60 caliber Kentucky rifle, its barrel having been trimmed by several inches and a larger than normal stock added.

A dozen yards behind the man, tethered in a string, were seven pack animals all bearing heavy loads consisting of long wooden crates. Close-by stood a saddle horse.

"Any luck, Lambert?" the man at the fire asked.

"None," the rider responded, reining up and sliding to the ground. He walked over to the fire, tucked his rifle under his left arm, and extended his fingers toward the welcome warmth. "That damn fool probably got himself killed."

"I hope not."

Lambert snorted. "We don't need that idiot, Newton. I say good riddance to the stupid son of a bitch. In all my born days I've never met anyone so incompetent."

Taking a seat, the man called Newton regarded his companion critically. "You're not using your head, partner. We do need Kennedy."

"Why do we need that simpleton?"

"Because he has the money and the business contacts. We don't."

"What's to stop us from making them *our* contacts?" Lambert asked.

Newton sighed. "We've been all through this already. Kennedy was in business for over ten years. He knows all the right people and has a reputation as an honest businessman. The ones who sell the goods to him wouldn't give us the time of day."

"I hate having to rely on him," Lambert groused.

"And you think I like it?"

Lambert gazed upward. The snow had tapered to a trickle. "I suppose we should continue searching for him," he said reluctantly.

"The sooner we find Isaac, the sooner we can reach the Utes," Newton mentioned.

"And the sooner we get our pelts," Lambert added, grinning. "Then we'll have more money than either of us could make in a lifetime of trapping lousy beaver. We won't know what to do with it all."

The stocky Newton grabbed his rifle and stood. "I know what I'm going to do with my share."

"Let me guess. You're going to St. Louis and bed a different whore every night."

"St. Louis, hell. I'm going to New York City. Whores there have class."

"A whore is a whore, Newton, and it doesn't make a difference whether she's in St. Louis or New York. Pay her price and she'll spread her legs."

"Shows how much you know. The whores in New York City wear nicer, fancier clothes with a lot of frills and lace and such. And they smell a hell of a lot better. Why, some of them take a bath every single day."

Lambert cackled. "Now I know you're pulling my leg. There's isn't a person alive who takes a bath every day. Once a year is more than enough. Take them too often and you wind up sickly."

"Have it your way," Newton said testily, adjusting

his hat. "But I've been to New York and I know what I'm talking about." He began kicking snow onto the fire and white smoke billowed heavenward.

"I didn't mean to get you riled."

"I'm not."

"I know better. I know that temper of yours."

"Drop it," Newton stated, kicking furiously. In a minute he had the flames extinguished and the smoldering embers soaked under a layer of snow.

Lambert walked to his horse and swung up. "Want me to take the north side of the valley and you can take the south?"

"We'll stick together," Newton said. "We're in Ute country now and we can't take any chances."

"They won't harm us."

"Only a fool would trust a savage," Newton stated. "If you're not careful you'll get your throat slit and your hair taken."

"Their chief gave his word."

"*One* of their chiefs made the deal with us," Newton corrected him. "The chiefs of the other villages would just as soon skin us alive."

"I'm not worried," Lambert declared. "We talked our way out of a scalping once and we can do it again."

"We were lucky, is all," Newton said. "Two Owls could have had us rubbed out any time he wanted." He paused. "I'm still not convinced he won't anyway once he gets what he wants."

"Are you saying we should turn around and head for the States after coming all this distance?"

"Of course not. We'd be crazier than loons to give up now."

"Let's go, then."

Newton went to the pack animals and took the reins in his left hand, then mounted his saddle horse. He took the lead, riding between the boulders and pausing once he was in the clear. The snow had practically stopped. His gaze drifted westward to a tranquil lake and the country on the far side. Suddenly he stiffened and asked, "Do you see what I see over yonder?"

Halting, Lambert took one look and smirked. "I'll be tarred and feathered. Who the hell would have a cabin way out here?"

"Let's find out."

Nate waited until Isaac Kennedy had greedily finished the bowl before broaching the subject of trapping again. He spent the time observing the greenhorn while Winona bustled about the cabin.

"A truly marvelous repast," Kennedy said at last, smacking his lips and staring at Winona. "My compliments to the lady of the house."

"My wife is an excellent cook," Nate commented. "But then, most Indian women are. They have to be."

"Why is that?"

"Because an Indian man doesn't want to take for his wife a woman who hasn't mastered the art of keeping a home. Cooking, sewing, the working of hides, the care of a teepee, all these are the responsibilities of the women."

"It sounds terribly boring."

"Someone who doesn't know any better would likely think so," Nate said testily, "but Indian women take pride in their work. In some tribes the women belong to special societies just like the warriors. They compete to see who can weave the prettiest patterns or who can cure the most number of hides. It's quite an honor for a woman to be considered the best at any task."

"But isn't it demeaning that the men get to go out and do the hunting and make war while the women do all the petty chores?"

"There's nothing petty about the work they do. The welfare and comfort of their families depends on them," Nate disclosed, annoyed at the man's attitude. "Besides, warriors never look down their noses at the women. They treat women with the respect they deserve."

Kennedy shrugged. "I guess I would make a terrible Indian."

"Do tell."

The portly man glanced at Nate's face and in the strained silence that ensued squirmed uncomfortably in his chair. "I didn't mean to offend you," he said at length. "And I didn't intend to insult the Indians, either. The good Lord knows I'm in no position to judge or speak badly of anyone."

"Oh?"

Kennedy abruptly rose and carried the bowl to the table. "Should I put this here?"

"Be my guest," Nate said, wondering what to make of the man's behavior. When Kennedy sat down he brought up the subject that most interested him. "You say that you plan to trap in Ute country?"

"Yes, indeed. Newton and Lambert know the way. I came along simply to watch over my investment."

"I don't understand. Did you foot the bill for the supplies?"

"The supplies? Oh, yes," Kennedy said. "I paid for everything."

"What kind of traps did you purchase? Newhouses?"

"I don't remember."

"How many pounds of powder and lead did you bring?"

"I'm not certain."

"What about flour and coffee?"

"We brought some."

"How much?"

"I don't know."

Nate's brow furrowed. For somehow who had fit out the trapping expedition, Kennedy knew precious little about the gear and goods purchased. "Well, I hope you know what you're doing."

"Why?"

"Because venturing into the heart of Ute country to trap beaver is about as dangerous as sticking your head in a grizzly's mouth to examine its teeth."

"I'm not worried. Newton and Lambert know what they're doing."

"Have they told you about the Utes?"

"Yes."

"Then you know that the Utes hate all whites? You know that they exterminate every trapper foolish enough to enter their territory? You know that next to the Blackfeet, the Utes are probably the most feared tribe in the northern half of the Rockies?"

Anxiety crept into Kennedy's expression. "Newton and Lambert never told me all those details."

"If I was you I'd think twice about carrying out your original plan. Head north a ways. There's plenty of prime beaver country and you won't need to worry so much about the Utes."

"I appreciate your concern, Nate, but we'll be all right. My friends know a Ute chief."

"Do you know this chief's name?"

"Two Owls."

A flood of memories washed over Nate. He'd met Two Owls himself several months ago and they had formed a temporary, uneasy alliance against the dreaded Blackfeet. Eventually they'd parted on friendly terms but he couldn't guarantee the Ute warrior would be so kindly disposed the next time they encountered one another. "How is it your friends know him?"

"They ran into Two Owls when they were trapping out here a few seasons ago."

"And they're still alive?"

"They talked him out of killing them."

It occurred to Nate that Newton and Lambert might be the biggest liars ever to don a pair of britches. There wasn't a trapper alive who could dissuade hostile warriors from taking their hair. The only reason he'd been able to hook up with Two Owls had been because he'd gotten the drop on the chief and refused to take his life. Out of a sense of gratitude or obligation, Two Owls had then helped Nate fight the Blackfeet.

Winona, who had moved over to the window, announced in Shoshone, "The snow is stopping, husband. I will go feed the horses more grass."

Twisting, Nate saw a few flakes trickling down and the sky beginning to brighten as the cloud cover moved eastward. "I will go."

"You should stay with our guest," Winona said, putting on her buffalo robe.

Nate hesitated. He didn't like the idea of her going out alone, but he decided against making an issue of it in front of Kennedy. "Okay. But be on your guard."

"Always," Winona said, smiling, and stepped to the door.

"Where is she going?" Kennedy inquired.

Nate faced him. "To feed our horses."

"You have horses? Is there any chance I could borrow one to go find Newton and Lambert?"

"We'll go together in a while," Nate proposed, unwilling to lend a precious horse to someone who had lost his own. He heard the latch slide open as Winona prepared to depart, then tensed when she gasped loudly.

Kennedy, who had his eyes on the entrance, blurted, "Oh, my!"

Rising, Nate spun to see a tall man in a brown coat standing just outside the cabin with a rifle trained on his wife.

Chapter Six

Nate instantly made a grab for one of his flintlocks but the newcomer's sharp warning prevented him from drawing.

"Try it and the squaw dies!"

Furious, Nate froze with his fingers almost touching the pistol. He watched the man motion Winona to move back and he followed her inside.

Isaac Kennedy jumped from his chair. "Lambert, what is the meaning of this outrage? These people saved my life!"

Another, stockier, man appeared in the doorway. This one wore a black coat and had a modified rifle in his right hand. He surveyed the interior briefly, then focused on Nate.

"What do you want?" Nate snapped, almost unable to resist the temptation to bring his flintlocks into

play. If only he could distract the one called Lambert!
The other man, he deduced, must be Newton.

"We were crouched below your window," Newton
said, pointing at the crack between the sill and the
flap. "We couldn't help but overhear parts of your
conversation with our partner, Mr. Kennedy."

"So?"

"So our partner talks too much."

Kennedy took several steps toward the two men. "I
don't understand. Why are you doing this?"

"Because you shot off your big mouth, jackass,"
Lambert stated.

"I told them nothing."

"Nothing and everything," Newton said, moving
over to the table to inspect the empty bowl put there
by Kennedy. "Is that buffalo stew I smell?"

No one said anything.

Newton glanced at Winona. "Take off the robe and
fetch me a bowl, woman, and be quick about it."

Instead of obeying, Winona defiantly stayed where
she was and glared at him.

"Do it or my friend here will shoot your man,"
Newton said.

Lambert looked at Nate and smirked.

Without hesitation Winona let the robe fall to the
floor, got a clean bowl from the cupboard, and
walked to the pot.

"I like a woman who knows how to listen," Newton
said. He chuckled and took a seat at the table, then
gazed at Kennedy. "I'm disappointed in you, Isaac. I
thought you had more brains than you do."

"But I didn't tell them a *thing!*" the portly merchant protested.

"You only think you didn't," Newton said. "But we
heard some of the questions this trapper was asking
you. You made him suspicious."

"I did? How?"

Newton sighed and rested his elbows on the table top. "Isaac, what are we going to do with you? Sometimes you are more trouble than you're worth."

"Sometimes?" Lambert echoed, and snorted contemptuously.

Nate's eyes flicked from one to the other as he impatiently waited for them to let down their guard. They both impressed him as being hard men, sinister sorts capable of slaying Winona and him without any provocation. Lambert, in particular, had the air of a wolverine eager to tear into its prey.

"Now then," Newton said, aligning his rifle on the table so the barrel pointed directly at Nate, "be so kind as to put those pistols of yours on the floor. And do it slowly or your woman will be seeking a new man."

Hesitating, Nate debated the wisdom of making a reckless attempt to cut both men down. He was certain he could drill a ball through one of them but the second would then send a ball into him. Winona would be on her own.

Lambert swung his rifle to cover Nate. "You heard my friend. Do it now, trapper."

Reluctantly, rage making his blood race, Nate slowly drew the right flintlock, then the left, and eased them to the wooden floor.

"Step away from the guns," Newton instructed.

Again Nate complied, his resentment knowing no bounds. His rifle was on the wall, his knife and tomahawk by the bed. Completely unarmed, he was at the mercy of the intruders.

Lambert came forward and took the pistols to the table, prudently keeping out of the line of fire. "Do we do it now?" he asked Newton.

"What's your hurry? We've just spent weeks trekking across the plains and into these mountains, trying our best to stay warm every foot of the way. We wasted over a day searching for Isaac while trying to

survive one of the worst blizzards I've seen in ages,"
Newton said. "I reckon we owe ourselves a treat. It's
warm in here and there's hot food. I say we stay a
while."

"And what about him?" Lambert inquired, nodding at Nate.

Newton drummed his fingers on the table. "What's
your name, trapper?"

"King. Nate King."

"King," Newton repeated, pondering. "Why do I
have the feeling I should know that name?"

At that moment Winona approached the table
bearing a bowl of stew and a wooden spoon. She kept
her features composed, betraying no trace of fear.

Newton stared at her protruding belly. "Your mis-
sus will be having her litter of half-breeds in four or
five months if I'm not mistaken, King," he said
sarcastically.

The insult cut Nate to the quick. He clenched his
fists and took a step but Lambert promptly covered
him.

"Hmmmmm," Newton said, deep in contemplation. He took the bowl and eagerly began eating.

"Hey, what about me?" Lambert asked.

"After I'm done I'll watch them and you can fill
your stomach," Newton proposed.

Winona returned to the fireplace and stood beside
the pot with the ladle in her hand, her gaze resting on
her husband.

For over a minute not a word was uttered. The only
sounds were the crackling of the flames and the
slurping noises Newton made as he ate.

Isaac Kennedy wore a bewildered countenance.
He stared at his partners, looking from one to the
other repeatedly. Several times he opened his mouth
as if to speak but changed his mind.

The man in the brown coat finally broke the
silence. He glanced at the south wall, where a dozen

traps hung, and wagged his Kentucky rifle at Nate. "Nice traps you've got there, King. Newhouses, aren't they?"

Nate simply glowered.

"Newhouses are the best around," Lambert went on mockingly. "If we were fixing to trap our pelts we'd take yours along."

Kennedy found his voice. "I don't want these kind people harmed," he said softly.

Lambert laughed.

"Did you hear me?" Kennedy addressed Newton. "We should up and leave now. This has gone far enough."

Belching, Newton pushed the bowl aside and beamed at the merchant. "Isaac, leave this to us. We've lived in these mountains off and on for the better part of ten years. We know what we're doing."

"If you hurt them our deal is off," Kennedy blustered nervously.

Newton leaned back and laced his hands behind his neck. "We haven't traveled this far to call it off now, Isaac. Not when we're days away from becoming rich men."

"I'll take the pack animals and go back to Missouri."

"I'm sorry, Isaac, but we can't allow you to do that."

"How will you stop me?"

Lambert chortled.

"Need you really ask?" Newton responded.

Total horror etched itself in Kennedy's face. He swallowed hard and exclaimed, "Dear Lord in heaven."

"I want you to understand," Newton said. "A chance like this comes along once in a lifetime for men like Lambert and me. We can't let it pass us by. If we called this off, you could always go back to owning a store and making a comfortable living. But Lambert and me would have to go back to trapping or whatever other backbreaking jobs we could find." He paused and frowned. "You can see my point, can't you?"

"I can see we're in the wrong here."

"City types!" Lambert declared bitterly. "It just proves that you can educate a fool but it doesn't mean he can think."

"I know I don't want to be party to a killing," Kennedy stated.

Newton stood and went over to the portly man. He placed his right hand on Kennedy's shoulder. "If there was any other way, I'd do it. But what if someone starts to ask questions later? What if the Army gets involved? If word should reach Fort Leavenworth there might be an investigation. Then suppose an officer was to show up here and this trapper was to tell him about these three men who came by in the dead of winter heading for the middle of Ute country. How long do you figure it would be before the Army put two and two together and was on our trail?"

Gnawing on his lower lip, Kennedy looked at Nate and Winona. "I didn't realize—."

"Of course you didn't. You let us handle this situation our way," Newton said.

Nate had listened to the exchange with an intense curiosity in the hope of learning the exact nature of their business with the Utes. Clearly they weren't planning to trap beaver. He well recognized the fate Newton and Lambert had in store for Winona and him. Outnumbered and covered, there wasn't much he could do. But he wasn't about to roll over and be murdered without a fight. If he had to, he'd charge Lambert and try to grab the pistols from the table.

Kennedy placed his right hand over his eyes and bowed his head. "What have I gotten myself into?"

"Don't fret yourself," Newton said. "You were all

for the enterprise back in Ohio when I first brought the idea up. You like the idea of having ten thousand dollars or more just as much as we do. Why don't you take a stroll outside? Maybe walk down to the lake?"

Nodding, Kennedy lowered his hand and moved toward the door.

Suddenly Nate saw an opportunity to turn the tables. The portly merchant inadvertently walked between Lambert and him, momentarily screening him from Lambert's view. Newton was staring at Winona. In that split-second Nate hurled himself forward, sweeping Kennedy aside with a powerful thrust of his arm and barreling into Lambert, grabbing the rifle barrel in one hand and Lambert's throat in the other.

Nate's momentum carried both of them into the table. Lambert recovered from his shock swiftly and tried to wrench the Kentucky free. They rolled to the right, off the table, and crashed onto the floor with Lambert on the bottom. Nate drove his right knee into the man's groin and Lambert screeched and tried to double over.

"Nate! Behind you!"

Winona's warning impelled Nate to let go of Lambert and roll again, to the right once more. It was well he did. The heavy stock of Newton's rifle swished through the very space his head had occupied a heartbeat before. Twisting, he saw Newton towering above him and swept his legs into the bastard's shins, knocking Newton backwards.

Newton stumbled against the table, waving his arms in an effort to retain his balance.

Surging erect, Nate felt a fleeting weakness induced by his many wounds but he disregarded the sensation and planted his left fist on the tip of Newton's chin. His foe swayed and Nate followed through with a right that buckled Newton's legs.

For a moment Nate had the upper hand.

Then Lambert rose, his face a beet red, and slammed his rifle barrel across the back of Nate's head.

Propelled forward, staggered by the cowardly strike, his senses swimming, Nate tripped over Newton and fell onto the table. He felt Newton's arms wrap around his legs and start to pull him down. Vigorously shaking his head to clear it, he glimpsed someone moving past him and shifted to find his wife brashly rushing Lambert with the ladle upraised to hit him in the face.

Snarling, Lambert struck her across the forehead with the rifle and Winona dropped on the spot.

"No!" Nate bellowed, his wife's plight fanning his fury. He pushed off the table and tried to kick loose from Newton even as he twisted and swung wildly at Lambert.

Shuffling aside, still in pain from Nate's kick, Lambert evaded the blow.

A fist rammed into Nate's gut and he bent over to flail at Newton. He rained three punches before the stocky cutthroat yanked him off his feet and he fell face down.

Isaac Kennedy was prancing about frantically in the background yelling, "No! No! No!"

Nate tried to rise again but Lambert stepped in close and delivered a kick to his ribs. Excruciating agony flared in his chest. He sputtered, still game, and put both hands on the floor. Another kick sapped all of his strength. He went limp and barely heard Newton growl two words.

"Do it."

Rough hands seized Nate's shoulders and he was flipped onto his back to gaze up at Lambert's feral features. The Kentucky rifle materialized above his face. He could see the barrel pointing at his forehead, could see the dark muzzle opening mere inches away, and he desperately jerked his head to the left at the very instant a tremendous explosion occurred, searing fire scorched his skin, and everything abruptly went black.

Chapter Seven

The bone numbing cold awakened him.

Nate opened his eyes and promptly wished he hadn't. His head throbbed with waves of pain, his chest ached terribly, and the bites itched unbearably. He gazed at the ceiling, commingled relief and astonishment at being alive sweeping through him. Suddenly he thought about Winona and impulsively attempted to push off the floor.

A veritable avalanche of anguish rocked his head.

Involuntarily crying out, Nate lay still and waited for the agonizing pulsations to cease. He took stock. The dim light in the cabin convinced him the time must be close to evening. Either that, or he'd been unconscious for who knew how long. His mouth and throat were as dry as a desert.

Of all his discomforts the pervading cold became the most bothersome. His skin broke out in goose bumps and he shivered uncontrollably. What had happened to the fire?

Nate slowly twisted his head to gaze at the fireplace. Sure enough, the blaze had long since gone out. He looked toward the entrance and discovered the door hung wide open. No one else was in the cabin.

The sons of bitches had taken Winona!

Grunting, he tried once more to sit up. The pain overwhelmed him. He closed his eyes and waited it out. When he could think straight again he tentatively raised his right hand to his face. His skin was sore to the touch and his fingertips became smudged with black powder. He realized he'd sustained powder burns when the rifle went off.

Girding himself, Nate lightly ran his fingers over his forehead and temples. On his right side, level with his eye, he found the start of a quarter-inch deep furrow that ran the length of his head. Merely touching it made him flinch. Apparently the ball had gouged him severely, then passed into the floorboards. A fraction deeper and he wouldn't have survived.

Nate slowly endeavored to sit yet again. His head rose several inches but jerked up short, his long hair seeming to be caught on something. He reached behind him and his palm pressed onto a sticky puddle. Blood, no doubt. His blood. Tracing its outline, he found a wide pool that had nearly dried.

Exercising care, he grasped his hair and proceeded to tug it loose. The movement aggravated his gunshot wound but couldn't be helped. Gradually the strands came free and he could sit upright.

Vertigo attacked him as he straightened. He rested, gazing right and left, enraged at seeing the pantry had been ransacked. Scanning the interior, he made another distressing discovery.

The Hawken was gone.

Nate scowled and got onto his knees, his head shrieking in protest the entire time. Taking a few deep breaths, he then stood, reaching out to the table for support.

Both flintlocks were also gone.

He stayed put for several minutes, noting all the items missing besides the guns and food. The powder he normally kept in a far corner had been stolen, as had his supply of lead. Several spare blankets stored on a shelf not far from the bed were gone. His traps still hung on the wall and the pots and pans he'd purchased for Winona hadn't appealed to the killers.

Nate took a cautious step, then a second. Snail-like, he crossed to the fireplace and picked up the wooden stick that substituted as a poker. Jabbing an end into the embers, he probed and poked until he located a hot spot. He took a handful of tinder from the small pile Winona stockpiled to the left of the fireplace and dropped the dry twigs in. Leaning down, his left arm braced on the wall, he huffed and puffed until the tinder caught. Adding a few small logs, he soon had the fire going again.

He admired his accomplishment for a minute, enjoying the warmth the flames radiated. Dizziness struck him once more and he moved haltingly to a chair to sit down until the uncomfortable feeling dissipated. How long would the attacks persist? he wondered. He couldn't afford any delays, not when Winona was in the clutches of hardened killers.

Or was she?

A shocking thought occurred to him. What if Newton and Lambert hadn't abducted her? What if—and a ripple of stark fear flowed along his spine— she was lying outside in the snow, dead?

Nate straightened and walked to the entrance. A gust of wind chilled him as he surveyed the ground and a fine spray of white mist hit his face. Practically everything was white; the trees, the boulders, the logs, the undergrowth, and the ground. The mantle of snow was two and a half feet deep and made finding tracks ridiculously easy.

There they were, right in front of him. Nate readily distinguished Winona's slender moccasin prints from those of the men. All four sets bore to the right. He did the same, neglecting to take his coat in his anxiety.

The trail led to the pen, which was empty. Nate found where Winona had mounted her brown mare and where his other animals had been added to a string the cutthroats possessed, bringing the grand total of animals being led to ten.

Why so many?

Deciding he didn't have the time to waste in idle speculation, Nate went into the cabin and closed the door. He scoured the room for weapons, finding only his knife and tomahawk lying under the bed. Either Winona had hidden them there or the killers had not needed them. Probably the latter, he figured, since Winona must have believed he was dead.

Nate strapped the knife around his waist and tucked the tomahawk handle under the belt. He slipped into his Mackinaw, found his hat, and moved to the door. Common sense told him to wait until he'd recovered his strength, but every minute he took to recuperate meant Winona got that much further away.

He reached for the latch when a peculiar thing happened. The door began swirling around him, going faster and faster, and his body started tingling all over. He tottered rearward, swinging his arms about to find support of any sort.

A veil of darkness abruptly enveloped him and he felt himself crashing to the floor.

* * *

"I don't see why you had to bring her along," Isaac Kennedy groused for the umpteenth time since leaving the King homestead.

Newton, riding ahead of the portly merchant and the Indian woman, glanced back in irritation. "Would you rather we shot her?"

"No."

"Then shut your trap," Newton advised, and gazed past the woman to where Lambert led the pack string. He faced due west, seeking the easiest passage through the forest, avoiding dense thickets and clusters of boulders.

"What do you plan to do with her, Ike?" Kennedy inquired.

"I'm fixing to make a present of her."

"Who would—," Kennedy began, then blurted out, "you wouldn't!"

"Why not? Two Owls will be right pleased."

"Damn you, man, she's pregnant."

"Noticed, did you?" Newton responded, grinning. "That only makes it better."

"How do you figure?"

"First of all, she's a Shoshone. The Utes are always raiding the Shoshones to steal horses and women. They think highly of Shoshone bitches," Newton detailed.

Kennedy frowned.

"Second of all, even if Two Owls doesn't want to keep her for himself he can always swap her for a few horses or other goods. She's the perfect gift."

"It's not civilized, I tell you."

Newton gestured at the rugged countryside. "This isn't civilization, storekeeper. Out here a man does what he has to do to get by."

His cheeks flushing with anger, Kennedy dropped back to ride alongside their prisoner. He stared at her, admiring her beautiful features and the manner in which she nobly held her chin high. "I'm truly sorry," he said.

Winona gazed straight ahead.

"If I'd known this was going to happen, I never would have stopped at your cabin," Kennedy assured her.

She didn't answer.

"I know you can speak English," Kennedy said. "I heard you call out to your husband. Why won't you talk to me?"

Deigning to cast a reproachful glance at him, Winona stated curtly, "Your heart is small."

Confused, Kennedy did a double take. "As far as I know my heart is perfectly normal."

Winona gave him a look that left no doubt she equated him with horse dung. She wrapped her robe tighter around her body and rode a shade faster to get ahead of him.

Undeterred, Kennedy caught up with her mare. "What do you mean by my heart is small?"

From Newton came a contemptuous translation. "She means you're a coward, Isaac. Shoshones, and most other Indians for that matter, look down their noses at cowards."

Lambert, overhearing, laughed heartily.

Kennedy bowed his head in shame and rode in silence for a while. Every breath he expelled formed a small white cloud before him and his lungs tingled from the frigid air. The tips of his fingers, although well covered by thick gloves, became cold. He glanced at the Shoshone woman, marveling at the fact she wasn't in the least bothered by the inclement weather even though her face and hands were fully exposed to the elements.

Their party crossed a rise and wound into a narrow valley below.

"I guess I can't blame you for thinking poorly of me," Kennedy said softly, trying to come to grips with his conscience. "I would too if I was in your shoes."

"She doesn't care how you feel, Isaac," Newton interjected without bothering to look around. "If she had the chance she'd gut you wide open."

"Would you?" Kennedy bluntly asked.

Winona looked at him, her spiteful expression confirming Newton's statement.

"I've never had anyone hate me before," Kennedy commented, hurt by her eloquent rebuke.

"You'll grow accustomed to it out here," Newton declared. "Folks hate Lambert and me all the time."

"I can't imagine why," Kennedy said.

Twisting, Newton's eyes narrowed as he regarded the merchant. "Watch it, partner. No man insults me and lives to brag of the deed.

"I meant no offense," Kennedy replied quickly.

"No, you never do," Newton taunted him, swinging about again.

Isaac Kennedy clenched his left hand and almost made a remark he would surely regret. He checked his temper and gazed at the woman again. Newton was undoubtedly correct. She had no interest in anything he wanted to say, but say it he must if only to make her understand that he deeply regretted her husband's death. He'd never been party to a killing before and the guilt weighed heavily on his soul. "Winona?"

Predictably, she ignored him.

"Fine, then. Suit yourself. But I'm going to speak my piece whether you like it or not," Kennedy stated, and paused. "I had no idea what I was getting myself into when I agreed to Newton's proposal. You see, I'm not a man of violence. I've made my living as a merchant, which is about as peaceful a life as one can find. All I wanted out of this venture was to make a sizeable profit. Do you understand?"

Winona rode onward, her lips compressed.

"I was tending my store and minding my own business back in Ohio when Newton came in one day. He was on his way from New York City, where he'd just visited his sister, back to the frontier. He saw the beaver hats I was selling and happened to mention that he knew a way to become rich off beaver pelts if he could only find a financial backer for the goods he needed. Well, I decided to provide the money."

A clump of snow fell from a nearby tree with a swish and a thud.

"You see, I'd been working for years in the mercantile profession and never really gotten ahead. Oh, I had a thousand squirreled away for a rainy day or old age, but like any man I wanted more. Newton's proposal intrigued me. Here was a way to reap a thirty thousand dollar profit from one trip into the Rockies. That's ten thousand apiece. And if this trip is successful, there's a chance we can do the same thing next year."

"You're wasting your breath, Isaac," Newton stated, sounding annoyed.

"She deserves to know."

"Like hell she does. She speaks English, savvy?"

"What?"

"If you tell her everything, we'll have to do the same to her as we did to her husband."

"Oh," Kennedy said. He hadn't considered that.

On all sides lay a great quiet, as if every creature in the mountains had found a convenient shelter during the blizzard and was still deep in slumber. Half the sky had cleared of clouds and bright sunlight lent the snow a brilliant luster.

Newton abruptly halted, staring to the southwest.

"Why have you stopped?" Kennedy asked as he reined up. "Do you see some game we can shoot for our supper?"

"All you ever think about is food," Newton said.

Kennedy gazed to the southwest in casual curiosity and immediately stiffened in alarm. Perhaps a quarter of a mile away, on a hill, were two riders. "Are those Indians?"

"They sure are," Newton answered.

"Do you know what kind?"

"Utes."

Chapter Eight

Nate awoke with a start and sat up, the movement racking his head with torment. He seemed to be making a habit of this. He gazed at the window, shocked to see evening was descending. Rising, he glanced at the fire. Tiny flames were all that remained of the blaze he'd started earlier.

Now what should he do?

Perturbed, he opened the door and gazed out over the hoary landscape. Already long shadows criss-crossed the snow. In another hour darkness would claim the Rockies.

Damn.

Nate slammed the door. Sudden pounding in his right temple emphasized his foolishness. He staggered to a chair and sat down. As much as the very thought upset him, leaving now was out of the question. Tracking Winona's captors at night would be difficult, even with the tracks in the snow to aid him. The bitter cold alone would severely aggravate his condition.

He realized he had no choice. He must stay overnight at the cabin and begin the pursuit at first light. In a way, perhaps, the delay would be a blessing. A night of sleep would do wonders to invigorate him for the ordeal he must face in the morning.

Nate's stomach growled, reminding him he needed food. Since the pantry had been emptied, he must find it elsewhere. But he was in no condition to do any hunting.

Wait a second.

What about the buffalo stew?

He rose and hurried to the pot hanging above the embers, a smile his reaction at finding the pot a third full. The rotten cutthroats hadn't been as thorough as they figured. He stirred the contents with the ladle, finding the stew almost hard. But that was okay. Once he got the fire roaring and added handfuls of snow, the stew would be fit for a king.

Nate set about preparing his meal. In due course he had the fire crackling, the snow in the pot, the Mackinaw hanging on a hook, and he was standing next to the fireplace inhaling the delicious aroma of the boiling meat and vegetables.

Although he tried not to dwell on Winona, she filled his mind every second. He knew there were men vile enough to force themselves on even a pregnant woman, and he frequently shuddered as his imagination conjured the most horrible scenes conceivable. Each time he got a grip on himself and attempted to carry on, but a profound sorrow gripped his soul.

Snug and warm by the fire, he ate three bowls of stew, ate to the point where his stomach seemed ready to burst at the seams. He sat afterwards for hours staring morosely into the flickering red and yellow fingers, reviewing all the joyous experiences he'd shared with Winona. She'd brought him more happiness than he'd ever expected to know. If anything happened to her, he'd track those three bastards down to the far ends of the earth if need be to satisfy his thirst for vengeance.

He thought about tracking them, about the monumental difficulties entailed, and frowned. On foot he stood little chance of overtaking them any time soon. Somehow, he must acquire a mount.

The weather would help him, though, by slowing their party down. Horses tended to move much slower than otherwise in two to three feet of snow and the severe cold would hamper the animals as well.

Nate sagged in the chair, his chin dropping to his chest. His eyelids fluttered as sleep tried to claim him. Rising, he shuffled to the bed and collapsed on his back with a relieved sigh.

Soon slumber overcame him, and his last mental image before drifting off was of Winona.

"If only those Utes had bothered to speak to us," Isaac Kennedy mentioned while hunkered beside the campfire and rubbing his hands together near the flames.

"I told you before," Newton mentioned from where he sat on Kennedy's right, "we were lucky they up and vanished into the forest. For all we know, they might not have been from Two Owls' village."

"Is that bad?"

"How many times must I tell you the same thing?" Newton snapped. "Our deal is with Two Owls. If Utes from any other village catch us, they'll stake us out for the buzzards."

"How can we avoid these other Indians?"

"We can't."

"Can't one of you ride ahead, find Two Owls,

and bring him here? That would solve all our problems."

From the other side of the fire Lambert vented an oath, then said angrily, "The only problem around here is you, storekeeper. You flap your gums more than a bird flaps its wings."

Kennedy glared at the tall man. "I don't like it when you talk to me like that."

"And I don't give a damn what you like," Lambert growled.

"That's enough out of both of you," Newton declared. "I'm sick and tired of listening to all this bellyaching."

"It's not my fault," Kennedy said.

"You should never have come along," Newton responded. "In these mountains you're like a fish out of water. We could have handled the trade just fine without you."

"I couldn't stay in Ohio after all I invested in this enterprise."

"You would have been a lot more comfortable right now, and a hell of a lot safer, if you had."

Kennedy couldn't argue the point. Despite the roaring fire his backside and shoulders were chilly and the jerky they'd consumed for supper had barely whetted his appetite. Staying in Ohio would have been the smart thing to do. He didn't want to tell his partners, but the main reason he came along was because he didn't trust them as far as he could throw them.

He glanced to his left at the Shoshone woman, admiring her profile. She hadn't taken a bite to eat and refused a cup of coffee. Now she sat over a yard from the flames, her buffalo robe draped loosely over her slender shoulders, apparently unaffected by the freezing temperature.

"Hey, quit making cow eyes at that woman," Newton said jokingly. "She has no interest in you."

"I beg your pardon," Kennedy replied indignantly. "I wasn't making cow eyes."

"Sure you weren't. Hell, man, you've been eyeing her ever since we left the cabin. But if you even so much as touch her, she'll kill you."

Embarrassed by the accusation, Kennedy looked at the fire, feeling his cheeks flush crimson. "Why must you always be so crude?"

"You call it crude. I call it telling the truth. You're smitten with her, Isaac. It's as plain as the nose on your face. Don't feel bad about it, though. Happens to a lot of whites. They take one look at an Indian gal, at all that long, dark hair and those full lips, and they can't wait to dip their pork in the barrel."

Lambert cackled.

"Please. Stop," Kennedy said. "You'll hurt her feelings."

"She's a lousy squaw," Newton said. "She doesn't have feelings, not like white folks do. Indians aren't quite human."

"I don't believe that."

"Of course not. You have mush for brains."

Both Newton and Lambert laughed merrily.

Kennedy waited until they were done before commenting. "Nate King didn't believe Indians are less than human."

"Nate King was a jack—," Newton began, then abruptly tensed and snapped his fingers. "Son of a bitch! I remember now."

"Remember what?" Lambert asked.

"Don't you recollect when we were in St. Louis? We went to a tavern while Isaac tucked himself in early at the hotel."

"Yeah. So?"

"So we got to chatting with that old fart, that trapper who had been to the rendezvous last year."

"I remember," Lambert said.

"Then *think*, stupid. What did he tell us?"

Lambert shrugged. "Oh, he went on about all the drinking and whoring he did. And he bragged about the money he made from his furs."

"What else?"

After pondering for a bit, Lambert continued, "He told us about a fight that took place between that *voyageur* from Canada called the Giant and some guy the Indians called Grizzly Killer, a free trapper named—." He stopped, then blurted, "Son of a bitch! That was him!"

"Must of been," Newton said, nodding. "Geez, from all we heard, we were lucky to get the jump on him or we'd be pushing up flowers come Spring."

"He was a tough bastard," Lambert begrudgingly admitted.

"Was King someone famous?" Kennedy inquired.

"In these mountains he was," Newton answered. "That old-timer claimed King killed a grizzly bear with just a knife."

"Is such a feat possible?"

"No," Lambert said. "That old trapper was just spouting his mouth off."

At that moment all three men were surprised when their prisoner spoke up.

"My husband did kill a grizzly with a knife," Winona stated softly.

Newton glanced at her and chuckled. "Well, look who decided to join the conversation. I take it you don't much appreciate us speaking poorly of your husband?"

"Since all of you will soon be dead, your words don't matter."

Kennedy arched his back. "Why will we all soon be dead?"

"Because my husband will catch you and kill you."

Her statement provoked laughter from Lambert and a nervous titter from Kennedy, but Newton studied her face closely.

"Your husband is dead, squaw."

"Not true. You only think he is. But neither of you bothered to examine him. I did while you were busy stealing our food and guns. He was still alive."

"You're lying," Lambert said.

"Believe what you want," Winona said, her gaze on the fire. "You will learn the truth soon enough."

Kennedy saw his partners exchange startled looks and realized they both believed her. Inexplicably, a tingle ran down his spine.

"Even if you are telling the truth, woman," Lambert said, "your husband was on his last legs. He'll never come after us."

"He will."

"How can you be so damn certain?"

"Because he is my husband. Because he is Grizzly Killer," Winona said proudly, her eyes sparkling.

Newton suddenly stood and stalked over to her. He grabbed the front of her robe and peered into her eyes as if trying to see into the depths of her being. Finally he gave her a hard shove and shook a fist in her face. "Damn you, squaw. Damn you all to hell."

Winona sat perfectly still and composed.

Now Lambert also rose and stared along their back trail. "You really reckon he'll come?"

"If he's as good as they say he is, he will," Newton stated. "And our tracks in the snow will lead him right to us."

"But he's on foot."

"For how long? What if he had other horses loose somewhere, out foraging?"

Moving around the fire, Lambert glowered at Winona. "Were there other horses?"

She didn't respond.

"Answer me, bitch!" Lambert barked, and raised his right hand to slap her.

"No!" Kennedy cried, rising. "Don't hurt her."

"Give me one good reason why I shouldn't bust her head," Lambert said.

"Would Two Owls like your gift if she's all battered and bruised?"

Hesitating, Lambert hissed and reluctantly lowered his arm. "Smart, storekeeper. Real smart. You said the one thing that will keep her in one piece."

Kennedy sighed in relief.

"What do we do, Ike?" Lambert queried his stocky friend. "Let it pass and hope he doesn't show?"

"You know we can't," Newton said solemnly. He scratched his chin while stepping to the east, the breeze whipping his wolf tail. "We got a late start today and only traveled about seven miles, I figure. One of us could ride back to that cabin at dawn, check on Grizzly Killer, and catch up with the string by tomorrow night."

"It's the only way," Lambert said, nodding.

"I'll go," Kennedy volunteered.

"Will you put a ball in King when you see him?" Newton asked scornfully.

"No."

"Then don't be dumb. One of us has to take care of him." Newton walked to where his bedroll lay and rummaged in the blanket. "Low card goes?"

"Fine by me," Lambert said.

"Here are the cards," Newton announced, rising with a worn deck in his right hand. He placed them on top of the bedroll, backs up, and made a fan of the deck. "Do you want to pick first?"

"You can."

Without hesitation Newton scooped a card up and held it out for all to see.

"The ten of spades," Lambert said, and grinned. "Hell, that should be easy to beat." He stepped to the bedroll and leaned down, his hand poised to pick, then paused uncertainly.

"We don't have all night," Newton prompted.

Lambert selected a card and turned it over. The dancing flames revealed it to be a two of clubs. "You always did have all the luck," he muttered, dropping the card on the blanket.

"Look at the bright side," Newton said. "You're the one who gets to kill King if he's still kicking."

"Yeah," Lambert said. He chuckled. "And this time I'll do the job right."

Chapter Nine

The rosy rim of the sun had just risen above the eastern horizon when Nate emerged from the cabin, shut the door behind him, and began his pursuit. The frigid air pierced deep into his lungs, invigorating him. With the snow halfway up his thighs, every step required extra effort, aggravating the bites and the temple wound. He'd bandaged the nasty furrow using strips of cloth from an old store-bought shirt he'd brought from New York City. His beaver hat helped keep the bandage in place.

A pair of ravens glided overhead, one of them uttering a raucous cry. Sparrows flitted in a nearby tree chirping contentedly.

Nate walked to one side of the trail left by the vermin who'd taken Winona. His entire body ached and he could have used another week in bed to heal.

But now he had no intention of resting for more than a few hours at a stretch until his beloved wife was safe in his arms again. A grim smile touched his lips at the thought of what he would do when he found the men.

He rounded the cabin and pressed westward. Thankfully, the wind had died down as it often did in the morning. He wouldn't need to worry too much about frostbite.

Nate always liked the aftermath of a heavy snow, when the mighty Rockies were transformed into a strange, pillowy landscape straight out of a fairy tale. The sagging trees, laden with snow on every branch, resembled white mushrooms. Boulders normally stark and angular became smooth white mounds. And the hard ground, draped in its soft covering of white fluff, appeared inviting enough to dive into.

He touched the hilt of the knife and the tomahawk handle, wishing he had a gun. Perhaps, if he had the time later, he would make a lance or even a bow. Anything to even the odds.

The golden orb in the east climbed steadily higher as Nate trudged onward. The bright glare reflected by the snow caused him to constantly squint to prevent snow blindness. He went half a mile. A mile. The farther he went, the better he felt as his muscles limbered up. The exercise did wonders for his constitution.

Nate kept his hands in his pockets and his chin low, concentrating on the clearly defined tracks. Knowing Newton and company had quite a head start, he only occasionally glanced up at the trail ahead. So it was with considerable surprise that at one such point he spied a solitary rider approaching from the opposite direction.

He halted in astonishment and automatically moved to the north behind a tree. Had they sent someone back? Why? He shielded his eyes with his left hand so he could see better and studied the oncoming figure, who was several hundred yards off. With a start he realized the man was an Indian.

A Ute.

Nate flattened against the trunk and peeked at the warrior, who rode parallel with the tracks in the snow. For some reason the Ute was following the backtrail, his eyes on the prints and not the terrain surrounding him. That's what comes from overconfidence, Nate reflected. Since the Utes tended to view this territory as their own, they could be a mite careless at times.

He slowly drew the tomahawk and eased from sight. If he could get the Ute's horse, he could rescue Winona before the sun set. But taking the mount would be next to impossible. The Ute wouldn't relinquish the animal without a fight, and Nate had observed a bow in the man's hand and a quiver slung over the warrior's back. Together they gave the Ute a nearly insurmountable advantage. A tomahawk was no match for a bow and arrows.

Nate knew Indian youths were taught at an early age how to properly use a bow, and by the time they were full grown they could hit a target the size of a pumpkin ten times out of ten while firing from the back of a galloping horse.

The trail lay only ten feet away, but in the time it would take Nate to reach the warrior with the tomahawk, the Ute would be able to unleash two or three arrows. The trick, then, was to attack the warrior before the man nocked a shaft.

Nate racked his brain for a way of prevailing and finally an idea struck him that promised success if he was lucky. Squatting, he held the tomahawk under his left arm while he packed together a large snowball. The simplistic trick he would employ was as old as the hills, yet sometimes the old ways were the best.

Straightening, he pressed his back to the trunk and
waited. He wouldn't throw until the Ute was abreast
of the tree, and then he must move like lightning to
bring the warrior down.

An upsetting thought suddenly occurred to him.

The Ute was bound to spot the tracks he'd made
moving from the trail to the tree. The warrior would
instantly put two and two together and perceive there
was someone behind the trunk. As soon as he popped
out, he'd be changed into a porcupine with feathers
jutting out of his body every which way.

That wouldn't do.

Nate had to launch his snowball well before the Ute
spotted his tracks. Yet to do so increased the risk of
being seen. He risked a look-see and found the
warrior approximately two hundred yards away.

There wasn't much time.

The seconds seemed to crawl by.

At last Nate heard the soft thud of hooves as the
Indian's stallion approached. He gripped the snowball tightly. Now came the moment of truth. Should
he kill the warrior or try to take the man alive?

An unbidden thought abruptly bothered him.

What if the Ute was a member of Two Owls' village?
He owed a lot to the chief, after all, and didn't want to
do anything to antagonize him. But when he weighed
Winona's life in the balance, his obligation to Two
Owls must rate as secondary.

The warrior's stallion snorted.

Nate tensed. Had the horse detected his scent? No,
there wasn't a sufficient breeze. Taking a deep breath,
he eased his eyes to the edge of the trunk.

Riding casually along fifty yards distant, humming
softly, clad in buckskins and moccasins, the Ute was
alternately gazing at the trail and surveying the
forest. The bow rested on his thighs. On his left hip
was a knife. He held the reins loosely in his left hand.

Nate's nerves vibrated as he waited for the warrior to draw closer. Forty yards separated them. Then thirty. At twenty he hefted the snowball. At fifteen he saw the Ute suddenly look straight ahead and feared the man had seen his tracks.

The Ute unexpectedly whipped an arrow from his quiver even as he elevated the bow, and a fraction of a second later the string twanged and the shaft leaped through the air.

Only the arrow wasn't aimed at Nate.

Mystified, Nate glimpsed the streaking shaft as it sped in a beeline along the trail, passing his tree by a wide margin. He heard a thud attended by a peculiar squeal, and shifting to the other side of the tree he looked out to discover a jack rabbit smack dab in the center of the tracks, thrashing and convulsing with the arrow transfixing its wiry form.

Concentrating on his kill, the Ute rode past the point where Nate had veered off to the tree and dismounted. The warrior placed the bow on the snow as he knelt beside the rabbit and drew his knife.

Not one to waste a singular opportunity, Nate burst from concealment, his legs kicking up snow in a fine spray, the snowball in his right hand and the toma-hawk in his left. He covered only a yard before the Ute looked up and saw him.

Instantly the warrior's cat-like reflexes came into play. In a smooth motion the man let go of the knife and scooped up the bow, his left hand darting for the arrows perched in his deer hide quiver.

Nate covered five of the ten feet. He saw the arrow pulled clear of the quiver and he flashed his right arm back, then out again. The snowball flew from his chilled fingers, right on target.

In the act of nocking the arrow to his bow, the Ute was unable to evade the projectile. With a sticky splat the snowball struck him full in the face, the snow getting into his eyes and nostrils, and he instinctively wiped at his face to clear his vision.

No you don't! Nate thought, and reached the warrior, the tomahawk upraised. He swung with all his might, using the flat side of the weapon instead of the razor edge, striking the warrior on the head above the ear.

Stunned, the Ute crumpled.

Nate yanked the man's knife from its sheath and tossed it a few yards away. He stripped off the quiver, placed it on his own back, and picked up the bow. With the tomahawk in his right hand in case the Ute tried to interfere, he backed up to the Indian's mount.

The stallion shied nervously at Nate's approach, its nostrils flaring.

He spun and grabbed the reins in the same hand that held the bow. The powerful animal nearly tore them loose. He held on, though, and spoke in a soft, soothing voice. Gradually the stallion calmed down to the point where he swung onto its back without mishap. Tucking the tomahawk under his belt, he glanced at the warrior and nocked an arrow to the bow string.

The Ute was just sitting up, his hand clasped to his bruised head. He blinked, saw Nate, and surged to his feet.

Nate trained the arrow on the man but didn't pull the string back. He motioned with his head, indicating the warrior should move farther from the horse. The Ute reluctantly complied, glaring his animosity. When Nate was satisfied the man couldn't possibly reach him before he could wheel and ride off, he lowered the bow.

A string of harsh Ute words burst from the man's mouth.

Not knowing the Ute tongue, Nate shook his head

and employed his hands in making sign language. No one knew exactly which tribe had originated the practice of signing. Indian legends had it that sign language had existed since the dawn of time. Winona had taught him well. He could converse as readily now in sign as he could in English. "I have no wish to kill you. Stand where you are and you will not be hurt."

The Ute's response was short and to the point. "Horse thief."

"I am called Grizzly Killer. You have heard of me?"

Stiffening, the warrior studied Nate for a moment. "Yes. You have killed many of my people."

"They were trying to kill me!"

"Why are you stealing my horse?"

"I need it. Bad white men have taken my wife and stolen my horses. I must find these men and kill them."

The Ute pondered the revelation for a bit before moving his arms again. "How many men are there?"

"Three," Nate answered, then thought to ask, "What are you called?"

"Barking Dog."

Nate would have grinned if not for the fact he was well aware of the special significance Indians attached to names. An Indian child received its name soon after birth. The name selected might be that of a favorite animal of the parent, a noteworthy event that took place on the day the baby was born, or perhaps a name honoring a valorous deed the parent had once performed. While Indian women invariably kept the names bestowed on them at birth, the men often changed theirs to reflect a brave deed they personally accomplished, to commemorate their encounter with an unusual animal, or in observance of a special dream. There were exceptions, however. Any Indian born with a physical deformity was usually known more by a name that signified the deformity, such as Short Leg or Hump Back. Very few Indian children, though, were born deformed. "Do you know the mountain with twin peaks south of here?" Nate asked.

"Yes," Barking Dog responded. "We call them the Breasts of Life."

"Good. In two weeks I will deliver your horse at the small lake on the north side of that mountain. I will tie it to a tree on the north shore and you may get it then."

The Ute's brow knit. "You will not keep it?"

"No."

"And what is to stop me from waiting with many men from my village?"

"Nothing. But a man of honor would not commit such a wicked deed."

Barking Dog smiled. "For a white man you are very wise."

"My wife is Shoshone. Maybe her ways have rubbed off on me," Nate signed with a grin. "I am sorry I must take your horse. I threw your knife in the snow," he disclosed, pointing at the spot. "So you can make a lance for your walk back to your village."

The Ute glanced at the spot and saw the knife hilt jutting in the air. "You are very strange, Grizzly Killer. Most whites would kill me and be done with it."

"Which village are you from?"

Surprised by the question, Barking Dog cocked his head. "The village of Chief Eagle Horse. Why?"

"I was curious," Nate said, and started to turn the stallion.

"Wait," the Ute signed urgently.

"What?"

"Though you are stealing my horse, you spared my life. I owe you my life, and I can not take such an obligation lightly. I will repay you now so I can kill you if we meet again after you return my stallion."

Now it was Nate's turn to grin. "How?"

"I have seen your wife."

A lightning bolt coursed through Nate's body. "Where? When?"

"Yesterday. Spotted Wolf and I saw three white men and an Indian woman. They must be the bad whites and your wife. They are not more than half a day's ride from here."

"The woman was unharmed?"

"Yes. We watched them for a while, then Spotted Wolf went to our village to get more warriors while I followed their backtrail to see if there were more whites around."

"How long before Spotted Wolf returns?"

"Four sleeps at the most."

Nate looked into the warrior's dark eyes, silently conveying his gratitude, then whipped the stallion around and rode hard to the west. By nightfall Winona would be safe or else.

Chapter Ten

Lambert had gone over a mile when he found the tracks of a large horse emerging from the trees on the south. Since the hooves weren't shod it had to be an Indian mount. He reined up and looked over his shoulder, trying to spot Newton and the others, but they had long since vanished into the forest.

He had a decision to make. Should he continue to the King cabin or go warn his friend that savages were shadowing them? He decided to press onward. It was only one lousy Indian, after all, and he was going in the same direction. With luck, he'd slay the savage *and* finish off Grizzly Killer.

Gripping his Kentucky rifle firmly, he moved toward the valley where the King cabin was situated. Fear of an ambush prompted him to be extra alert. He constantly surveyed the woods ahead but saw only wildlife.

A few black-tailed deer regarded him from a hill to the north before fleeing into the trees. At one point a golden eagle soared overhead. And once a lynx bounded across the trail less than forty yards away.

Lambert covered two more miles. His mind started to stray as he thought about the unbelievable wealth that would soon be his. Ten thousand dollars! Maybe more depending on how good a bargain they struck with that crafty Two Owls. Never in his wildest dreams had he expected to possess such an incredible fortune. To him, or to anyone who barely eked out a living year after year, such a sum was a godsend.

To think that he owed his good fortune to the worst mishap that could befall any trapper; being captured by hostile Indians. If Newton and he hadn't taken a chance a year ago and ventured deep into Ute country to do their trapping, they never would have been captured by a war party of Utes. Then they would never have been taken to Two Owls' village and Newton would never have had the opportunity to make his desperate pitch to the chief.

Lambert chuckled. The most amazing moment in his life had been when Two Owls agreed to the deal. Of course, Newton had no intention of making good. His friend had made the proposal simply as a last-ditch means of saving their lives. In fact, one of the other Utes had been sharpening his knife to take Lambert's hair when the inspiration struck Newton.

Good old Newton.

They'd joked about their narrow escape all the way back to St. Louis, vowing never again to go anywhere near Ute country. Then Newton had taken it into his head to visit his kin in New York City, and on the way back had met Isaac Kennedy.

Now look at them.

Soon they would have more money than they could earn in nine or ten seasons of trapping. Soon they—.

What was that?

Lambert abruptly reined up as he spied a horseman far off to the east. The rider was moving at a reckless pace, his horse throwing up a wide wake of white spray. He hunched low over the pommel and moved into the trees on the right side of the trail. Dismounting, he looped the reins around a branch, cradled the Kentucky in his arms, and walked to the tree nearest the tracks. Concealed there, he peered out and studied the man, anticipating it would be the Indian who had been shadowing them.

His first observation was that the man rode a stallion. The sheer size of the horse precluded it being a mare. An Indian horse, he guessed, and gleefully anticipated putting a ball into the bastard's head.

Then he saw the hint of red in the man's coat.

Red?

As in a Mackinaw?

Lambert tensed, recalling the Mackinaw in the King cabin, hanging on the wall.

No, it couldn't be!

Even if the rotten squaw was right about her husband being alive, there was no way that King could be in pursuit so soon after being shot.

Lambert nervously licked his lips, his eyes narrowing. If that was indeed Grizzly Killer, then the man wasn't human. Lambert had seen the wound caused by his ball. He'd leaned down and laughed into King's face after shooting him. Blood had been pouring onto the floor.

That couldn't be Nate King!

Uneasy, Lambert watched the rider come ever closer. He saw the Mackinaw clearly, saw the big man astride the stallion, and swallowed a lump that formed in his throat. It *was* King.

He shook his head, dispelling his anxiety. So what if Grizzly Killer had survived? Another ball would do the trick, and this time Lambert intended to make doubly certain that the son of a bitch breathed his last before bearing the good news to Newton.

He checked the Kentucky, even going so far as to tamp the ramrod down the barrel to verify the ball and patch were properly placed at the bottom and ready to fire. Satisfied, he replaced the ramrod and cocked the hammer.

Let the Grizzly Killer come.

Lambert was ready.

He cradled the Kentucky again and leaned against the trunk, studying the lay of the land to determine how close he should let King get. Since he didn't want to miss, the closer, the better. Twenty to twenty-five yards should be about right. He noticed a tree on the north side of the trail that appeared to be about that distance off. Fine. When King came abreast of the tree, he'd shoot.

Hell, it would be easy.

Lambert grinned and idly observed King's rapid progress. The man was pushing the stallion to its limits, evidently in a hurry to reach his squaw. Lambert snickered contemptuously. He despised Indian lovers. To him, every buck and squaw in the West deserved the same treatment; extermination. No trapper or mountaineer would be safe as long as the Indians were allowed to exist. One day, he reasoned, the Indians west of the Mississippi would suffer the same fate as the Indians east of the Mississippi. They would either be killed off or driven from their lands. It couldn't happen soon enough to suit him.

King was now a quarter of a mile distant.

Crouching, Lambert braced the rifle barrel against the tree. He trained the sight on the approximate spot Grizzly Killer would be when he pulled trigger.

The cold air tingled his nose and made him want to sneeze. He pinched the tip of his nose together to nip the sneeze in the bud. Even the faintest of sounds sometimes carried far in the Rockies and he was taking no chances on alerting King.

He recalled the stories that old fart had related about Grizzly Killer. No less a personage than Shakespeare McNair, one of the premiere mountain men, had taken King under his wing and educated him in the ways of the wilderness. King was supposed to be a crack shot and utterly fearless. The Shoshones and the Cheyennes in particular held him in great respect. And the Blackfeet, it was rumored, wanted King's hair more than any other white man's because Grizzly Killer had been instrumental in helping a band of Shoshones defeat a war party led by a noted Blackfoot warrior.

King rounded a stand of small pines and came directly toward Lambert's position. Grinning, he held the Kentucky steady and lightly touched his finger to the trigger.

Any moment now.

Nate held his body close to the stallion, squinting to compensate for the bright glare of sunlight reflecting off the mantle of snow. He heard the arrows bouncing slightly in the quiver and hoped none would fall out. When he overtook the cutthroats he might need every single shaft.

His body pained him terribly but he ignored it. Every now and then his head took to throbbing. The agony would subside after a spell, though.

He scanned the trail ahead as he rode, seeing the line of tracks made by Barking Dog near those made by the party bearing westward. Then he noticed another set. Straightening, perplexed, he saw where a second set of prints had paralleled the trail for a considerable distance stretching back in the direction the killers had gone.

What did it mean?

As he drew nearer he discerned that this second set had angled away from the trail and into the trees to the south. Had Barking Dog lied? Had the other Ute accompanied Barking Dog this far and then headed for their village?

He glanced at the treeline, mystified, observing the sunlight glint off the tip of a thin horizontal branch. Simultaneously came the chilling realization that branches were incapable of reflecting sunshine.

Rifle barrels, on the other hand, could.

So superbly coordinated were Nate's reflexes that the very instant he saw the glinting object and perceived it to be a rifle, he threw himself from the stallion, diving to the right, and he was scarcely out of the saddle when the booming of the ambusher's weapon proved his instincts correct. Landing on his right shoulder, he rolled upright and sprinted toward the woods. Two arrows fell out as he rolled but the rest stayed in the quiver.

The stallion continued galloping westward, spooked by the rifle blast.

Nate reached a tree in five bounds and darted behind its bole. He crouched, slid an arrow out, and nocked it. Who was out there? he reflected, catching his breath and letting his racing blood slow down. Very few Indians owned rifles, and most of those who did were dwellers of the plains. Not more than a dozen Utes all told, he estimated, owned a firearm, which made the likelihood of his attacker being an Ute warrior extremely remote.

There was only one logical conclusion: Either Newton or Lambert had backtracked.

He peered out, searching the vegetation opposite for his adversary. A hint of motion prompted him to jerk his head back a fraction of a second before a rifle cracked and the ball smacked into the tree.

Whoever it was, the man could reload quickly.

Nate glanced over his shoulder, debating whether to seek sanctuary in the forest and make the killer come after him. If he had a rifle instead of a bow, he would naturally stand firm. But he'd not wielded a bow regularly since he was much younger and felt at a grave disadvantage. He stared at the shroud of smoke hovering beside the tree where the killer was concealed, wishing it would dissipate on the wind so he could see his enemy. Then it occured to him: If he couldn't spot the ambusher, neither could the man spot him.

Suddenly dashing to the right, staying bent at the waist, Nate ran from tree to tree, expecting to hear the boom of the rifle at any second. Traveling a dozen yards, he stopped behind a pine tree and knelt to study the forest on the other side of the trail.

There lingered enough smoke to partially obscure the trunk, but the left leg of the man bearing the rifle was in full view.

Nate raised the bow and sighted on the killer's limb. He breathed shallowly so the tip of the arrow would hold steady, then pulled the string back to his cheek, straining his arm to its limit. About to fire, he hesitated.

What if he missed? He would alert the ambusher to the fact he'd moved. Since he couldn't guarantee he could hit the leg, perhaps he should try to work his way around the man and come up on the killer from the rear.

He lowered the bow and continued running to the west. After twenty yards he halted and from the shelter of an oak tree checked on the ambusher. Beyond discerning an outline of the man's body, he couldn't identify who it was. The killer appeared to be concentrating on the tree Nate had vacated.

Now came the difficult part. He braced his legs,

tensed, and focused on a tree across the way. Once committed, he would be in the open for a good thirty feet. If Newton or Lambert spied him, there would be plenty of time for whichever one was trying to kill him to place a perfect shot.

Nate bolted, sprinting as quickly as humanly possible through the high snow, his progress retarded by the clinging white fluff. He didn't bother glancing toward the killer. Any distraction, however brief, slowed him marginally. Run! he mentally shouted at himself. Run like you've never run before.

To his utter amazement, Nate reached the sheltering woods without being shot. He squatted beside a pine and beamed at the prospect of gaining the upper hand. Exercising extreme caution, he advanced slowly toward the tree screening his foe. He moved in a crouch, waddling through the snow at times, always making certain there was undergrowth or a tree between him and the ambusher. Knowing the snap of a single twig would give him away, he was especially careful not to brush against any branches.

At last he drew within twenty feet of his quarry, pausing behind a waist-high boulder to tighten his grip on the arrow and the bow. All he had to do was jump up, aim, and let the shaft fly.

Nate straightened, the bow sweeping up, the arrow level. There stood the tree in question. There were the tracks in the snow leading from the woods to the tree, and the packed snow at the base of the tree that indicated the man had indeed been at that spot. But there were no tracks leading away and the killer himself was nowhere in sight.

Mystified, Nate moved around the boulder. Where could the ambusher have gone? Was the man employing the same tactic he'd just executed and now their positions were reversed? He scanned the forest but saw nothing.

Damn.

Nate stepped toward the tree, intending to search the area where he'd first gone to ground. He took several strides when he heard a distinct click to his rear and a mocking voice declared triumphantly:

"Make one move and you're a dead man!"

Chapter Eleven

Nate became a statue. The voice sounded close enough to convince him that if he tried going to the right or left, a ball would pierce his back before he could hope to whirl and fire.

"Wise man," the voice taunted. "Now drop that bow and put your arms in the air."

Frowning, Nate complied. He recognized the speaker as Lambert before he pivoted. The killer smirked and pointed the Kentucky at his chest.

"So we meet again. Fancy that," Lambert joked, coming to within six feet and halting. "I've heard of being hard to kill, but you're worse than any grizzly that ever lived. No wonder they call you Grizzly Killer."

"You know who I am?" Nate said to keep the killer chatting. Why hadn't Lambert simply shot him and been done with it?

"We figured it out," Lambert answered. "Actually, Newton did. Then that squaw of yours got to bragging about how you'd be after us before long and we decided one of us should come back and plant you in your grave real personal like."

"Have you harmed my wife?"

"Your squaw is fine, Indian lover. We're not about to lay a finger on her since we plan to give her to the Utes."

Anger made Nate clench his fists. "Put down that gun and we'll settle this man to man."

"That head shot must have addled your brains," Lambert said, and snorted. "I've got the drop on you and I intend to keep it until I'm ready to send you to meet your Maker." He wagged the Kentucky. "How does it feel knowing your life is in my hands?"

Nate didn't bother to answer.

"I could have killed you when you were trying to sneak up on me but I didn't want to spoil my fun," Lambert went on. "I'm fixing to take my time, make you suffer a little first."

"You're mighty brave when you're up against an unarmed man," Nate commented.

Lambert's gaze dropped to Nate's waist. "You're not exactly unarmed, are you? Use one hand and drop that knife and the tomahawk. And no sudden moves unless you want a ball in your head."

Easing his right arm downward, Nate tugged the tomahawk free and let it fall into the snow. He used two fingers and pulled the knife from its sheath.

Adopting a cocky attitude, Lambert nodded at the trail of tracks leading from the forest to the tree. "Pretty clever of me to walk backwards in my own footprints so you couldn't figure out where I'd gone, huh?"

"You're brilliant," Nate said, and started to lower the knife toward the ground, his eyes riveted to Lambert's. The killer laughed and blinked. It wasn't much of an opening, but it was all Nate was likely to get. Even as Lambert's eyes closed, he gripped the knife firmly and flipped it straight at the killer's face while hurling himself to the right.

Lambert fired, but he squeezed the trigger while ducking to the left to avoid the knife and the movement threw his aim off.

Nate felt the ball tear at the edge of his Mackinaw sleeve as it streaked past, and then he was bounding forward, taking the offensive, his arms extended. He slammed into Lambert, wrapping his arms around the man's waist, and they both went down, the Kentucky pinned between them.

Hissing like an enraged rattler, Lambert drove his knee into Nate's groin. The blow landed squarely and Nate almost released his hold to try and roll away. Sheer grit sparked him to swing his right fist into Lambert's jaw instead, rocking the man's head back. He planted a left, the combination sufficient to cause Lambert to sag, stunned.

Nate heaved to his feet, grabbing the Kentucky as he did and wrenching the rifle from Lambert's grasp. He tossed it aside. No sooner had he done so, however, than Lambert kicked him in the stomach, doubling him over.

"Damn you!" the cutthroat roared, and kicked again, sweeping his left foot into Nate's neck.

Staggered, Nate stumbled rearward.

Lambert swept upright, his right hand clawing for the flintlock adorning his waist. "I'll finish you off proper," he barked.

Ignoring his pain, Nate sprang just as the pistol swept clear of the belt. He batted the barrel away with his left forearm and rammed his right fist into his enemy's mouth, knocking Lambert backwards.

Again the trapper tried to bring the flintlock into play.

Nate pressed his initiative to keep Lambert off

balance, raining a flurry of blows to the man's face, battering him without let up. He pummeled Lambert to his knees, then slammed his own knee into Lambert's face.

Down the tall man went, still gripping the flintlock.

Pouncing on Lambert's arm to pin it to the ground, Nate tore the pistol from the man's grasp. No sooner had he done so, however, than Lambert desperately punched him on the throat. Had the swing been delivered with all of Lambert's strength, it might have crushed Nate's windpipe. As it was, Nate fell onto his right side, releasing the flintlock to clasp his neck, his features contorted in acute anguish, wheezing as he tried to breathe.

Lambert scrambled to his knees, then jumped on Nate and tried to clamp both hands around the younger man's neck.

Although short of breath Nate resisted furiously, blocking Lambert's hands and trying to return the favor by seizing the killer's neck. They grappled and rolled, their faces inches from one another, with Lambert's teeth exposed in an almost bestial snarl. They were evenly matched and the battle raged on for over a minute with neither one gaining an edge.

Nate hurt everywhere. Try as he might he couldn't prevail, and to make matters worse they rolled into a large tree, his spine absorbing most of the impact. He had to let go, gasping for air.

Pushing erect, Lambert back-pedaled and began scouring the snow for the flintlock.

Nate wasn't about to let him find it. Gritting his teeth, he shoved to his feet and charged. Lambert turned to meet him and tried to connect with a punch, but Nate evaded the man's flashing arm. They warily circled each other, seeking an opening they could exploit.

Blood seeped from Lambert's crushed lips. He licked them and spat, his gaze never leaving Nate's face. "I'm going to skin you alive," he stated, the words slightly distorted.

"First you have to beat me," Nate retorted.

In a savage onslaught Lambert attempted to do just that, making up in brute strength what he lacked in finesse. He flailed away, trying to beat Nate into the ground, but most of his blows were countered.

Blocking the strikes made Nate's arms ache horribly. He cast about for a stout limb he could employ as a club or *anything* that would serve as a weapon. A few feet to the left was a narrow, tapered hole in the snow where a heavy object had been tossed and sank down. Was it the flintlock? Praying such was the case, he summoned a reservoir of stamina and punched. One of his uppercuts scored, tottering Lambert rearward.

Whirling, Nate dived at the hole and thrust his eager hands into the frigid snow, his fingers exploring for the flintlock. Instead, he touched slender cold steel and his right hand drew forth his butcher knife.

Lambert shouted out in victory.

Twisting, Nate saw the killer raising the flintlock from the snow. The man's thumb curled around the hammer and started to pull it back. "No!" Nate cried, bounding at his adversary, the knife hilt clutched in his right hand.

Elevating the flintlock, Lambert grinned.

Nate was still a foot away when the tall man squeezed the trigger and they both heard the loud ticking sound of the flint as the firestone struck the steel pan. But there was no loud retort; the black powder didn't ignite. It was a misfire, undoubtedly caused by wet snow fouling the piece.

Because Nate was already moving at top speed, including his right arm which was spearing toward Lambert even as the killer pulled trigger, there was no time for Nate to alter the sweep of his hand, even if he wanted to. A heartbeat after the flintlock misfired, his knife sank to the hilt into Lambert's chest with a muted thud.

Lambert stiffened and jerked backwards, the useless pistol falling from his trembling hand, his eyes widening, shock transforming his face into a pallid mask.

Nate released the knife and stood still, watching his enemy carefully.

"Damn you," Lambert exclaimed, taking the jutting hilt in both hands. He braced and heaved, extracting the blade cleanly, but in doing so he permitted his life's blood to gush forth like a geyser, the crimson fluid spraying out from his chest and splattering his clothing and the snow at his feet.

There were no words for Nate to say. He clenched his fists and waited for the inevitable.

"Dear Lord," Lambert breathed, flinging the knife down. He pressed his palms to the slit, vainly endeavoring to staunch the pumping blood. Gripped by sudden dizziness, he fell to his knees. "I'm dying," he wailed. "I'm dying."

Nate's features hardened.

"Help me!" Lambert blurted frantically. "Please help me!" He made as if to reach for Nate, but the action only allowed the blood to gush faster. "Please!"

"Good riddance."

Lambert was too terrified of the Grim Reaper to be mad. He coughed, red spittle rimming his lips, and doubled in half. "This can't be!" he stated. "I'm not ready to die."

"Few ever are," Nate said, retrieving both the flintlock and his knife.

Lambert coughed again, violently, and leaned down until his forehead rested in the snow. "I feel so weak, so cold."

Satisfied the man no longer posed a threat, Nate

went about collecting all their weapons. He held the Kentucky and smiled. It wasn't a Hawken, but it would suffice for the job at hand. He went back to Lambert and listened to the killer's labored breathing.

"Grizzly Killer?"

"Yes?"

"My head is all fuzzy. I can't seem to think straight."

"It won't be long now."

Lambert twisted to look up. Blood was trickling from both corners of his mouth. "Will you do me a favor?"

"Depends."

"I—I have a sister in Ohio. Cincinnati. Her name is Christine Lambert. Will—will you get word back to her?"

Frowning, Nate hesitated. Why should he do a favor for someone who had tried to kill him and stolen his wife?

"Please, King. Write her a note, a line, anything," Lambert pleaded, his voice quavering, his words barely audible. "She's the only kin I have. I don't want her worrying on my no-good account."

About to say no, Nate saw tears rimming the mountaineer's eyes. A pool of blood soaked snow had formed under Lambert's chest. "All right," he said, and sighed. "I'll send a line back East with the first person I meet who is heading to the States."

Lambert smiled wanly. "Thank you," he said sincerely, and stiffened, uttering gurgling noises, his tongue protruding as he tried to suck in air. He attempted to speak one last time but produced an inarticulate grunt. His body sagged, his eyes locked wide open, and he ceased breathing.

Nate waited a moment before stepping forward to verify the man had died. He wasted no time removing

Lambert's ammo-pouch and powder-horn. Rising, he scoured the forest for the killer's mount and spied the horse screened in the timber. He took several strides, then halted and glanced over his shoulder. Should he bury Lambert or simply leave him? Shrugging, he continued to the horse.

The Almighty had made carrion eaters for a reason.

Ike Newton had abruptly reined up and stared thoughtfully eastward. "Did you hear that?"

"Hear what?" Isaac Kennedy asked, stopping. He was in the lead. Behind him came the Shoshone woman, then Newton with the string.

"I thought I heard a shot."

"I heard nothing."

"You wouldn't," Newton snapped. He glanced at Winona. "Did you?"

"My husband has killed your friend."

Newton rode forward until he was beside her. "You don't know that. You're just trying to rattle me."

"I know," Winona said softly.

"Bull," Newton declared, moving ahead of both of them, sick to death of Kennedy's company and wishing he'd never decided to take the squaw along as a gift for Two Owls. He looked back once more, wondering if the bitch was right. Naw. She couldn't be. Lambert had killed a couple of dozen Indians and whites in his time. He felt certain his friend had taken care of Grizzly Killer.

They were moving slowly up a steep slope toward a narrow pass between two snow covered mountains. Once beyond the pass they would be in a valley where Two Owls wintered.

Newton idly scanned the shimmering peaks around them and spied a soaring hawk far off. He thought about the Ute chief and wondered whether the savage would double-cross them. If so, there wasn't a damn thing they could do about it. They'd simply have to take Two Owls at his word and hope for the best.

He glanced at the Shoshone, pondering her devotion to the man called Grizzly Killer. She was a squaw, but she also possessed the kind of traits he most admired in a woman. What would it be like to be loved by someone like her? How did some men rate such sterling wives while others wound up with shrews? Secretly, he envied Nate King. If a fine woman had ever loved him, he might have amounted to something. A good woman's love, he'd once heard a traveler at a tavern say, could make the difference between a happy life and damnation.

Sighing, Newton cradled his Kentucky and focused on the pass. The depth of the snow increased the higher they went, and their horses were finding the going difficult.

"Ike?" Kennedy spoke up.

"What now?"

"Suppose she's right. Suppose Lambert is dead."

"He's not."

"But just suppose he is. Maybe we should release her."

"Don't you ever give up?" Newton stated testily.

"Hear me out. If King *is* after us, we serve our own best interests by letting her go. Once he has his wife back safe and sound, he'll leave us alone."

"No, he won't."

"Why not?"

"Because men like Nate King aren't the kind to overlook a little thing like being shot and left for dead and having their wives taken. If it takes Grizzly Killer the rest of his born days, he'll track us down."

They lapsed into an uncomfortable silence until they attained the pass, a gap no more than eight feet wide. There the snow lay only nine or ten inches in depth, thanks to the sheltering influence of the two mountains. On both slopes were huge boulders caked with snow.

Newton reined up and waited for the others to join him. The squaw came up on his left, Kennedy the right. He gazed eastward and was surprised to spot a lone horse far in the distance galloping in their direction. "What the hell!" he blurted.

Stopping, Kennedy twisted in his saddle and looked. "Is that's Lambert's horse?"

"It's impossible to tell at this range," Newton said, although he believed the animal to be larger.

Kennedy's eyes narrowed. "There's no rider."

"I noticed."

"What does it mean?"

"I don't know," Newton said, watching the horse plow steadily onward.

"Should one of us go catch it?"

"Isaac, you ask too doggoned many questions," Newton barked. He hesitated uncertainly, and at that moment a chilling sound emanated from the left-hand slope, a sound every mountaineer dreaded.

It was a low, guttural growl.

Shifting, Newton glanced at the white slope and felt his blood turn to ice at beholding an enormous panther perched on top of a boulder a mere twelve feet away. Even as he laid eyes on the big cat it snarled and leaped at the Shoshone woman.

Chapter Twelve

Mounted on Lambert's horse, Nate continued his pursuit. He had the bow and the quiver rolled up in a blanket behind the saddle. The reloaded Kentucky was in the crook of his right arm. And the flintlock had been added to the knife and tomahawk adorning his waist.

The fight had taken a lot out of him. He felt alternately weak and strong, clear-headed and slightly dizzy. As much as he longed to rescue Winona, he must not push himself excessively hard for fear of passing out again. He concentrated on staying with the trail, holding the horse to a steady but not rapid pace.

The tracks left by Barking Dog's fleeing stallion were freshly defined in the snow, and from the length of its gait it appeared the animal had no intention of slowing any time soon.

Nate forged ahead, alert for more Indians or his quarry. The trail was winding toward a pair of mountains miles off. From the extensive trapping he had done in the area during the fall, he knew a pass existed between those peaks and beyond it lay a valley where game was plentiful.

The thought of game reminded him about food and made his stomach rumble. He debated whether to stop and decided not to waste precious time hunting. There would be ample opportunity to eat after he rescued Winona.

As he rode his mind drifted. He speculated as to whether he'd made a blunder by settling in a cabin situated so remotely. If he took Winona to St. Louis, for instance, they'd be a lot safer during the winter months. But the trips back and forth would be extremely taxing, and they'd be compelled to deal with the ugly specter of bigotry. There were plenty of whites who despised Indians, no matter which tribe they belonged to. And if something should happen to him while there, Winona might find herself alone in a strange city and forced to rely on the kindness of total strangers.

He'd previously given serious consideration to wintering with Winona's tribe. The Shoshones would be delighted to have them in their village during the colder months. Except for the ongoing raids by the Blackfeet and the Utes, there would be little danger.

However, he had to confess that he preferred to stay right where he was, in their cabin. Yes, they were at the mercy of the elements. Yes, they were in constant danger of attack. And yes, they could well starve. But the cabin was their *home*, and he'd rather take his chances there than anywhere else.

The time passed slowly. The brightness of the snow hurt his eyes and made them water.

What if he went snow blind? A chronic ailment of trappers who spent winters in the Rockies, snow blindness often came on suddenly and sometimes took up to a week to go away. The only cure was resting and staying indoors in subdued light. Even then, those who recovered complained for a long time afterward that everything they looked at was enveloped in a reddish haze.

To go snow blind now would doom Winona to captivity among the Utes and force him to try and return to the cabin. He squinted, making his eyes thin slits. The less light that struck them, the lower the risk of injury.

The time seemed to crawl by.

He still had a couple of miles to go before reaching the two mountains when a faint retort reached his ears from the vicinity of the pass. His pulse quickened. Newton and the others must be in trouble, which did not bode well for Winona. He goaded Lambert's horse to go faster and forgot about keeping his eyes narrowed against the glare.

Rarely seen by Indians and mountaineers, the largest cats in the Rockies were known for their reclusive nature. Often over seven and a half feet long from the tip of their nose to the end of their tail, they sport a tawny coat with small dark patches on the backs of their tapered ears and accenting their whisker patches. These cats were referred to as panthers by the majority of the trappers. A few called them catamounts. Others used the French word for such felines, calling them *couguars*, while some had taken to speaking of the huge cats as mountain lions.

By any name they were trouble when aroused or hungry, and no one knew this fact better than Ike Newton. Seven years ago, while trapping near Sweet Lake, he'd tangled with a panther that had tried to take a beaver caught in one of his traps. He'd managed to scare the critter off with a shot from his pistol. But this time he couldn't afford to miss.

At the moment the panther launched itself into the air, Newton was bringing the Kentucky up while thumbing back the hammer. With the squaw between the cat and him, he didn't have much of a shot. He simply elevated the barrel in the general direction of the hurtling beast, pulled trigger, and hoped for the best.

The panther's tapered claws were within a foot of Winona's face when the heavy lead smacked into the cat's brow. The hit fell right between its slanted eyes and flipped the animal rearward in a tight loop. Its two hundred and fifty pound body crashed down into the snow head first and it lay perfectly still.

A few of the pack horses shied, compelling Newton to grip the lead tightly.

Winona hadn't so much as budged. She simply stared at the dead cat, her features stone-like.

"I say!" Kennedy blurted. "That was remarkable shooting, Ike."

"I was lucky," Newton responded gruffly, annoyed at how close he'd come to losing his gift for Two Owls.

The storekeeper edged his mount nearer to the cat. "I didn't know panthers attacked people."

"Ordinarily they don't," Newton confirmed. "I figure it was going for her horse and she was just in the way." He snickered. "Which is a break for me."

Kennedy glanced at him. "I don't understand."

"Now I don't need to worry about the squaw sticking a knife in my ribs while I'm sleeping. She won't do a damn thing to me."

"Why not?"

"Because I just saved her life, you idiot, and Indians are real particular about such things. Save a buck or a squaw and they owe you for life. And if they happen to be your enemy in the first place, then they can't kill you until they repay the favor," Newton said, and laughed merrily. "I could hand her a gun and she wouldn't even shoot me."

"An excellent suggestion," Kennedy declared. "Considering the dangers in this wilderness, she should have the means to protect herself."

"Isaac."

"Yes?"

"I'm not *really* fixing to hand a gun over to her."

"But you just said—."

"Move out," Newton barked, and did just that, taking the lead. He would have been better off shooting Kennedy, he irately reflected. Newton had traveled almost to the end of the pass before remembering that his Kentucky was empty. Stopping, he moved back to the first pack horse and removed Nate King's loaded Hawken from the blanket in which he'd rolled it before departing the King cabin. He stuck the Kentucky in the pack and examined the Hawken.

He'd heard generally favorable reports about Hawkens. Manufactured by Jacob and Samuel Hawken of St. Louis, they were reputed to be highly reliable and extremely accurate in competent hands. Their only drawback was their weight. A few trappers who had purchased Hawkens later sold the rifles because they were too heavy to be toting all over the Rockies. This despite the fact that Hawkens were much shorter than conventional long rifles, the typical Hawken having a thirty-four inch barrel while the average Kentucky sported a barrel of forty-four inches.

There was one other advantage Hawkens possessed over the Kentucky and Harper's Ferry rifles. Hawkens used the newfangled percussion system of firing instead of relying on the spark of a flint on steel to ignite the black powder.

He hefted the rifle, liking its sturdy feel, then

realized the Shoshone was glaring at him. Without looking at her he wheeled his horse and resumed their journey.

It took them a while to work their way down from the pass to the valley below. The going was slippery and several of the pack animals nearly lost their balance. Once on level ground they rode rapidly toward a stream and followed the winding ribbon of water into a dense forest.

Newton felt on edge. He had no guarantee that Two Owls' warriors wouldn't shoot on sight and there was always the risk of running into Utes from another village since their hunting ranges tended to broadly overlap. To compound the danger, Blackfeet war parties frequently invaded Ute territory. Running into those devils would decidedly ruin all of his well laid plans.

He glanced up at the sky and glimpsed the afternoon sun through the canopy of limbs overhead. If Lambert didn't return by nightfall, then he would be inclined to believe the squaw; his friend truly had been rubbed out. If so, *he* could expect Grizzly Killer to show up sooner or later, probably sooner. A man whose wife had been abducted seldom dallied when seeking vengeance.

For the next several hours they walked deeper into the long, sinuous valley, heading toward the far end some twenty miles distant where they might find Two Owls' encampment. The snow under the trees lay to a depth of two feet or more and the pack horses at times had to struggle through higher drifts up to their chests. No one bothered to speak during all this time. Each of them was immersed in thought. Winona rode with her back straight, her chin jutting defiantly. Kennedy frequently gazed at her when he felt certain she wouldn't notice. Occasionally he would cast a dark look at his partner.

The sun hung just above the western horizon when Newton finally raised his right hand to call a halt as they were entering a wide clearing on the south side of the stream. "This is where we'll camp," he announced.

"At last," Kennedy breathed, sliding to the ground near the water. He surveyed the vast, wild domain of Indians and wildlife and sighed. "When will we find Two Owls?"

"How should I know?" Newton responded, waiting for the squaw to dismount before doing the same. "We'll find him when we find him."

"Someone who didn't know better might swear you don't have the foggiest idea where to locate him."

Newton took an angry stride toward the storekeeper, then drew up short in disgust. "This isn't the civilized East, Isaac. It's not like New York City or Ohio where you can make a business appointment, then sit down at the appointed time to discuss selling or swapping your goods. I told Two Owls I'd look him up after I got the items he wants. For all he knows, I'm not even coming." He paused. "Frankly, I was shocked when he agreed to let us go. He must really want the merchandise."

"Of course he does," Kennedy said. "He'll have more than all the other tribes combined. Why, he could even prevent the Blackfeet from invading his territory."

"Prevent them, hell. He can march on up to Blackfoot country and drive the bastards clear into Canada."

Winona, who had been listening with interest to the discussion, glanced at the wooden crates. There were four on each pack animal, bringing the grand total to twenty-eight. "What are in those?" she inquired.

Newton snorted. "Well, look who's decided to be

civil." He jabbed a thumb toward the crates. "It's none of your damn business what's inside those crates, and if I find you poking around where you shouldn't be, I'll slit your throat. Savvy?"

"Yes."

"You wouldn't slit her pretty throat, would you?" Kennedy asked apprehensively.

"I sure as hell would. Killing squaws and bucks is the same as killing any animal."

"But Indians are people, the same as us."

"Indians are nothing like us, idiot," Newton stated harshly. "They're heathens, plain and simple. Didn't you hear what President Jackson said? He called Indians an inferior race who should be pushed aside to make room for us whites."

"I read an account in the newspaper," Kennedy said.

"There you have it. When the President of the United States, no less a man than Old Hickory, calls Indians inferior, then they're damn well inferior," Newton snapped. "It's our duty as white men to rub every last one out."

Kennedy stared at the crates. "Is that one of the reasons you're trading with Two Owls?"

"Hell yes. He'll use these to wipe out every enemy he has, and those enemies are mostly other tribes. We're doing our part to reduce the Indian population."

"You said 'mostly'," Kennedy noted. "Won't Two Owls use them against trappers also?"

"Probably," Newton said with a shrug. "But it will serve any trapper right for being stupid enough to be caught by the Utes."

"But you were caught by the Utes once."

"Don't quibble, Isaac. Why, if President Jackson knew what we were up to, he'd likely give us a medal."

"Then why are you worried about the Army finding out?"

Newton hefted the Hawken and scowled. "You ask too damn many questions. A man has got to learn when to keep his mouth shut out here or he'll wind up eating lead." He nodded at the horses. "Get busy watering and feeding our critters."

"Why don't you do it?" Kennedy responded indignantly.

"Because one of us must keep an eye on the squaw to see she doesn't try and slip away," Newton said. "And since I couldn't trust you to watch a tree stump, I get the job."

Scowling, Isaac Kennedy sullenly proceeded. But as he worked he cast many a side-long glance at Ike Newton, the sparks of ripening hatred blazing to life in his eyes.

Chapter Thirteen

The sun hung above the western horizon when Nate's vision first blurred briefly, causing him to rein up and blink rapidly as tears of discomfort washed over his pupils. He had just made it safely through the high pass and down the slippery slope. The sight of the dead panther had brought immense relief; the dead cat explained the shot he'd heard earlier and tended to indicate Winona was still safe.

Now he wiped the back of his left hand across his eyes and gazed at a narrow stream in front of him. The landscape came into sharp focus again, prompting a sigh of relief. For a second there he'd figured he was coming down with snow blindness.

He urged Lambert's horse onward, sticking to the trail left by Winona and her abductors. Soon the sun would set and he'd be unable to track them. As much as he despised the very idea, he would need to halt for the night. Knowing that his precious wife was somewhere in the tract of forest just ahead made him all the more eager to overtake the scoundrels and save her.

Nate paralleled the stream and entered the trees. A hint of movement drew his attention to the northwest. There, grazing on a thin strip of brown grass he exposed, was Barking Dog's stallion. Evidently the animal had followed the scent of the other horses until hunger compelled it to eat. Recalling his promise to return it if possible, Nate approached the big animal cautiously, fearing it would bolt.

The stallion simply munched and scarcely paid attention to his presence.

Sliding to the ground, Nate walked over and gripped the stallion's Indian-style bridle. A length of rope had been looped twice in the middle around the horse's lower jaw to form a lark's-head knot that served as the bit, leaving the ends free for use as the reins. He patted the animal's neck and uttered soft words, then undid the knot and removed the bridle. Making a single loop at one end, he slipped the loop over the stallion's head, clasped the other end, and climbed back into the saddle.

Turning Lambert's horse, Nate resumed his pursuit. He realized he must find a suitable spot to camp soon or darkness would catch him stranded in the trees. There was plenty of water but he had to find ample food for both animals before he could rest for the night.

The upper rim of the sun was barely visible when he finally found a small open space bordering the stream and called it quits for the day. He guessed Newton and company to have at least a five mile lead, probably more. If not for the deep snow he would have caught up with them by now.

Nate let the horses drink a little, then went into the forest and searched for vegetation. He kicked the snow aside at various points, exposing the ground underneath, until he found an area overgrown with weeds and brown grass. Clearing off a ten-foot circle, he stood by and idly watched the animals eat. As he stood there his vision blurred for the second time.

Panicked, he barely breathed until once again everything became crystal clear. Why did it keep happening? he wondered. He was glad night would soon descend, giving his eyes relief from the shimmering snow cover.

A loud rumbling in his stomach reminded him of his own need for food. After all the wounds he'd sustained, he couldn't afford to go for long without eating. Yet if he waited for the horses to get their fill, it would be too dark for him to shoot accurately. Accordingly, he tied both animals to tree limbs bordering the cleared space and walked into the undergrowth to find game.

Only then did the difficulty of his task become apparent. The heavy snow had driven the majority of wild animals into their dens, burrows, or heavy brush. Few creatures other than birds were abroad. He walked hundreds of yards and saw only a few sparrows.

His stomach growled again. Nate halted beside a towering pine tree to scan the landscape. The sun had disappeared and already the amount of light had diminished by a third. To compound the situation, the air was rapidly becoming colder. He cradled the Kentucky in his elbows and began to make a loop back toward the horses. As he passed a thicket he registered movement out of the corner of his left eye and peered into the tangle of thin, barren branches to discover a white rabbit moving slowly out the far side.

Instantly Nate snapped the rifle to his shoulder,

Join the Western Book Club and GET 4 FREE* BOOKS NOW!
A $19.96 VALUE!

Yes! I want to subscribe to the Western Book Club.

Please send me my **4 FREE* BOOKS**. I have enclosed $2.00 for shipping/handling. Each month I'll receive the four newest Leisure Western selections to preview for 10 days. If I decide to keep them, I will pay the Special Members Only discounted price of just $3.36 each, a total of $13.44, plus $2.00 shipping/handling ($19.50 US in Canada). This is a **SAVINGS OF AT LEAST $6.00** off the bookstore price. There is no minimum number of books I must buy, and I may cancel the program at any time. In any case, the **4 FREE* BOOKS** are mine to keep.

*In Canada, add $5.00 shipping/handling per order for the first shipment. For all future shipments to Canada, the cost of membership is $16.25 US, which includes shipping and handling. (All payments must be made in US dollars.)

NAME: _____

ADDRESS: _____

CITY: _____ **STATE:** _____

COUNTRY: _____ **ZIP:** _____

TELEPHONE: _____

E-MAIL: _____

SIGNATURE: _____

cocked the hammer, and took a bead on his potential supper. He steadied his arms before squeezing the trigger. At the booming retort the rabbit flipped into the air and landed on its side, then thrashed about on the snow, staining the cover crimson, before it expired.

Elated, Nate barged through the thicket and scooped the mammal up. He couldn't wait to sink his teeth into a roasted piece of meat. Spinning, he hastened back to the horses. The darkness intensified more every minute. Verifying the animals were all right, he decided to let them continue grazing and went to the small clearing beside the stream. He bustled about gathering limbs and soon had a roaring fire going. The welcome warmth brought a smile to his lips.

Skinning and preparing the rabbit took less than five minutes. Next he erected a makeshift spit over the fire. After finding two forked branches, he imbedded the bottom end of each into the ground, one on either side of the flames. He used his knife to smooth down and sharpen a long, slender, straight branch and inserted the tip through several chunks of rabbit meat. Then, after suspending the straight piece between the forks, he squatted and watched in anticipation as the crackling fingers of red and orange licked at the meat.

The delicious aroma made his mouth water. He greedily licked his lips and turned the spit occasionally to prevent the meat from burning. All the while his stomach did its best to imitate an enraged grizzly bear. When finally satisfied that the meat had been roasted long enough, he deposited the Kentucky at his side and lifted the long branch.

His nose tingled and his lips quivered as he raised the meat to his mouth. The rabbit was hot to the touch, but he took a bite anyway. Slowly, savoring the taste, he chewed the mouthful and swallowed. He inadvertently looked into the fire, thinking to himself that he'd never eaten such flavorful rabbit, and unexpectedly his vision blurred for the third time.

Nate immediately closed his eyes and swung his head away from the bright flames. Both of his temples pounded painfully as he waited for the sensation to subside. Dear Lord! What would he do? He'd be at the complete mercy of the elements and any wild animal that came along without his sight. Not to mention poor Winona's certain fate if he failed to save her.

After a bit he tentatively cracked his eyelids and felt monumental relief at being able to see perfectly once again. Keeping his back to the fire, he proceeded to polish off the rest of the meat on the spit. It barely whetted his appetite. Accordingly, he slid several more chunks onto the sharpened branch and carefully aligned it on the forked limbs while keeping his gaze averted from the flames.

Feeling renewed, his insides wonderfully warm, Nate started to stretch when he heard a sound that turned his blood cold.

Both Lambert's horse and Barking Dog's stallion started neighing in terror.

Isaac Kennedy was furious, both at himself and his recently acquired business associate. He was mad at himself for going along with such a hare-brained, get-rich-quick scheme when he should have known better. And he was mad at Newton for a variety of reasons, not the least of which was the trapper's condescending attitude and demeaning remarks.

Back in Ohio, when Newton had first proposed the idea, the mountaineer had behaved like a proper gentleman. But after they journeyed to St. Louis and were joined by Lambert, Newton's attitude changed, becoming one of open sarcasm. Lambert had only aggravated the situated and fueled Newton's underlying contempt. Now Isaac knew that both men had despised him. They saw him as a blithering incompetent.

How dare they!

He was the one who had put up the capital for their venture. *He* was the one who had obtained the merchandise needed to conduct trade with the Utes. *He* was the one who had dropped everything and left the comfortable life to ensure their success.

The ungrateful sons of bitches.

As Kennedy sat on the east side of the fire contemplating the injustice done him, his gaze strayed to the lovely Shoshone woman off to his left. He'd never known an Indian woman before, never realized how truly beautiful they were. The mere sight of her stimulated him in a way he hadn't been stimulated in ages. He secretly watched her, his gaze lingering on her exquisite face. Every now and then he would look lower and frown.

Seated on the west side of the campfire, absently gnawing on jerked venison, Ike Newton was also staring at the Shoshone, only he did so openly and with malice etching his expression. "It appears you were right, squaw," he declared bitterly. "If Lambert was still alive, he'd have caught up with us by now. Which means your husband likely killed him."

Winona said nothing, her eyes fixed on the inky wall of vegetation bordering the clearing.

"Lambert was the best friend I ever had," Newton went on. "I'm not about to take this lying down." He touched the Hawken lying across his lap. "I aim to pay Grizzly Killer back."

"You would be wise to let me go and leave this country as fast as your legs will carry you," Winona said. "If you don't, my husband will hunt you down."

"Let him come, bitch."

Kennedy stiffened. "That's no way to talk to a lady."

"Lady?" Newton repeated, and chuckled. "Indian women are little better than whores, Isaac."

"They are not."

"What the hell do you know? Have you ever lived with a squaw?"

"No."

"Ever bedded one, even once?"

"Of course not."

"Then don't go getting on your high horse unless you've been in the saddle. I bet you don't know that trappers at the rendezvous can practically buy any Indian woman they want."

"What do you mean 'buy' them?"

Newton laughed. "You're a storekeeper. You're supposed to know all about buying and selling and stuff like that." He paused. "I'm telling you that trappers can buy Indian girls for a day, a month, hell, even a year if they want. A few yacks, like King, marry them."

"I don't believe you."

Leaning forward, Newton clenched his fists and glowered. "No man calls me a liar and gets away with it."

"I'm sorry. I didn't mean to say you weren't telling the truth."

"It sure sounded like that to me."

Kennedy deliberately refrained from meeting the trapper's stare. He glanced down at his right side where his rifle lay propped on his bedroll. "I've been meaning to ask you, Ike. Would you do me a favor?"

"What?" Newton responded in surprise.

"I still don't have the hang of loading my gun. Either I don't add enough powder or I forget to wrap a patch around the ball. Would you load it for me? If we run into hostile Indians I want to be prepared."

Newton muttered a sentence under his breath, only a few words of which were audible, something to the effect of "waste of manhood." Then he sighed and nodded. "Sure. I'll load your piece for you. Bring it here."

Grabbing his rifle, Kennedy rose and walked around behind Winona to hand the gun to his partner. "Sorry I'm so scatterbrained, Ike."

"We can't all be Daniel Boone," Newton said, referring to the Pennsylvania-born frontiersman who had died only eight years before yet whose exploits were already legendary. He stood and methodically commenced reloading the storekeeper's rifle using his own powder-horn and taking a ball from his own ammo-pouch.

Kennedy stood patiently to one side, observing. His eyes darted to the Shoshone woman twice. He clasped his hands at his waist and nervously twined and untwined his fingers.

"The trouble with you and most Easterners," Newton said as he worked, "is that none of you were ever taught how to fend for yourselves. You've grown so accustomed to buying whatever you need to live, you can't even provide the necessities. Why, if you ever found yourself stranded in the Rockies, you wouldn't last two days."

"I suppose not," Kennedy said, gnawing on his lower lip.

"It's not your fault," Newton said, removing the ramrod from the portly man's gun so he could shove the ball and patch down the barrel. "I blame your parents. Any father who doesn't teach his kids how to live off the land, find water and kill game, isn't much of a father in my book."

"You're absolutely right, Ike," Kennedy said, glancing to his left at the sizeable pile of broken branches he'd gathered earlier for use as firewood during the night.

"I doubt anyone in New York City even knows how to skin a deer," Newton rambled on while sliding the ramrod down the Kentucky. "At the rate things are going, in fifty years no one will be able to make do for themselves."

"Deplorable," Kennedy stated. He tentatively stepped toward the pile. "I think I'll add another limb to the fire."

"Just one," Newton advised. "If we use too many now, you'll have to go out in the middle of the night and collect more."

"I wouldn't want that to happen," Kennedy replied, and leaned down to select the stoutest branch he could find. Holding it in both hands, he stared at his partner's back and gave the branch a practice swing.

"Your rifle is loaded," Newton announced, replacing the ramrod. "Try not to blow your foot off."

"I won't," Kennedy said, sliding up behind the trapper and raising the branch on high. Then, ever so politely, he said, "Ike?"

"Yeah?" Newton responded, pivoting.

The storekeeper swung the branch with all his strength, putting his entire weight into it. His blow caught Newton squarely on the forehead and spun the man around. Newton fell where he stood, the Kentucky slipping from his limp fingers, his hair within inches of the flames.

Quickly Kennedy discarded the club and scooped up the Kentucky rifle. As fast as he was, though, the Shoshone almost beat him to the punch. The instant Newton fell, Winona made a move toward the Hawken lying near his feet. Kennedy swung the Kentucky toward her and shook his head. "Stop!"

She paused, her arm outstretched toward the rifle.

"The last thing in the world I want to do is hurt you," Kennedy told her, "but I will if you force me.

Until you prove that you can be trusted, I can't let you get your hands on a weapon."

Winona frowned, her gaze lingering on her husband's gun.

Not taking a chance, Kennedy kicked the Hawken aside. "All right. I want you to get the horses ready. We're moving out."

"You want to travel at night?"

"Yes. I plan to deliver the merchandise to Two Owls myself, and the sooner we get going, the sooner we'll reach his village. Once I have the beaver furs he promised, I can head back to the States a rich man."

"Why take me along? You can do it yourself."

"I'm afraid not. I need someone who can interpret for me."

"But I don't speak the Ute tongue."

"Newton told me all about Indian sign language. So get cracking with the horses."

Straightening, Winona gazed westward. "You are taking a great risk. Two Owls agreed to trade with Newton and Lambert, not you. He might take your crates and have you scalped. And it is certain the Utes will never let me leave their village."

"You let me worry about Two Owls," Kennedy said. "Don't fret yourself about the Utes keeping you hostage, either. I have a plan that will keep you out of their clutches."

"And then what? Will you take me back to my husband?"

Kennedy hesitated before answering. The corners of his mouth tilted upward when he spoke. "You have my word that once we're done with the Utes, I'll take you back."

Ike Newton unexpectedly groaned.

"What about him?" Winona asked.

"What indeed?" Kennedy rejoined. He stepped to the Hawken, tucked the Kentucky under his left arm, and bent over to retrieve the shorter rifle. Cocking the hammer, he moved to the trapper's side and pointed the barrel at Newton's head.

"You would shoot a man who can't defend himself?" Winona inquired.

Kennedy had never killed anyone in his life. But he thought of the thirty thousand dollars he stood to gain and the bonus besides if he played his cards right, and he had no trouble at all pulling the trigger. The recoil made the Hawken jerk in his hands. He looked down through the gunsmoke and grimaced at the mess the ball had made of Newton's face.

Winona was silent, her expression grim.

"Put this rifle on one of the pack animals," Kennedy directed, and tossed the Hawken to her. She caught it and walked toward the tethered string.

Far in the distance a wolf howled.

Grinning, Kennedy gazed up at the stars and inhaled the crisp air. Instead of feeling remorse over killing Newton, he felt invigorated. So this was what it felt like to stand on one's own feet! For perhaps the first time in his life he'd taken his destiny into his own hands and he felt marvelous. Glancing at Winona, who was moving among the pack animals, he hefted the Kentucky and chuckled. Ike had been right all along.

Fending for one's self was the only way to live.

Chapter Fourteen

Nate raced through the gloomy forest toward the horses, the rifle in his right hand. Both animals were still whinnying in fright. He had ten yards to cover when a feral snarl reached his ears. Increasing his pace, he crashed through the brush and burst from the woods into the clearing.

Both horses were trying to pull free, their great hooves stamping the ground, their ears pricked and their eyes wide.

The source of their fear was crouched on the east side of the open space. A large lynx, a cat not half the size of a mountain lion but equally savage if cornered, hissed at Nate the second he appeared, then wheeled and bounded into the undergrowth.

Nate let it go. He watched the thickly furred body and stubby tail disappear in the darkness before going to the horses to calm them. Since it would be virtually impossible for a lynx to bring down a full grown horse, he assumed the cat had merely been curious. From accounts related by other trappers, he knew that lynxes typically subsisted on birds, rodents, and the remains of dead deer or moose. Occasionally they would bring down a starving or sickly deer, but for the most part the larger mammals were beyond their capability to subdue.

He calmed both horses and led them back to the campfire. Halfway there he stopped short at the faint sound of a shot coming from much farther up the valley. He cocked his head, waiting for a second retort, but heard none.

Logic dictated that Newton or Kennedy must be responsible. Why had they fired? He doubted they were hunting game so late. Could they possibly mean the shot as a signal for Lambert? If so, they were doomed to be terribly disappointed.

He secured both animals and sat down to finish eating the rabbit. The chunks he'd placed on the spit were quite well cooked. He dug into them relishing the meal, and only when the last edible portion of the rabbit was sliding down his throat did he lean back, smack his lips, and wipe his greasy hands on his buckskins. For good measure he belched.

Nate was careful not to stare at the fire, even indirectly. His eyes seemed to have recovered. Now all he needed was a good night's rest and he'd be after those bastards in the morning.

He reluctantly rose and gathered spare wood to be used before dawn. After accumulating a sufficient quantity, he scooped out the snow down to the ground within a foot of the flames. Taking the blanket Lambert had carried in a roll tied behind his saddle, he spread it in the hole, then settled down on his back and nestled the rifle against his right side.

Nate closed his eyes and listened to the crackling of the fire and the whispering of the wind. As fatigued as he was, he expected to fall sound asleep within minutes. But this wasn't the case. His mind raced of its own volition, reviewing the incident at the cabin and the subsequent events with startling clarity.

He rolled onto his side, thinking the change of position would enable him to finally doze off. Try as he might, though, he couldn't get the image of Winona in Newton's clutches out of his mind. Surely even a scoundrel like Newton wouldn't lay a finger on a pregnant woman, he assured himself. But the assurance rang false.

Opening his eyes, he gazed up at the stars. Deep down he blamed himself for Winona's predicament. Had he been more vigilant back at the cabin, had he not accepted Kennedy with open arms and thus allowed himself to be distracted, she wouldn't be in their hands.

He'd completely forgotten two rules of thumb passed on by his mentor, Shakespeare McNair. As one who had spent the greater portion of his life in the wilderness, Shakespeare knew best how to survive. The old mountaineer was a veritable fount of wisdom, and Shakespeare had said, quite somberly, "Out here a man can't afford to let his guard down for a minute. If you want to last, you must amend the golden rule a mite. Love your enemies, but always remember to keep your gun loaded."

Truer words had never been spoken, Nate reflected. Of course, sometimes the mountain man made no sense whatsoever, such as the time Shakespeare had said, "If a man hasn't made any enemies by the time he's thirty-five, then he can pretty much chalk up his life as a failure." What the hell was *that* supposed to mean?

He rolled over on his other side and shifted his weight. The idea of not even bothering to sleep occurred to him. If he saddled up right away, he might overtake Winona by morning. But he's also likely to be so tuckered out that he wouldn't be worth a hoot against Newton. The trapper was bound to be a tough customer in a pinch. Kennedy, on the other hand, didn't worry him in the least. If ever a totally harmless specimen of manhood had been born, the portly storekeeper was the one.

Gradually his mind wound down. He roused himself once to feed more branches to the fire and check on the horses, then he settled back down and, in no time flat, he was snoring away. Even in sleep, though, his anxiety made itself known. He dreamed a horrifying dream in which his beloved wife was ravaged repeatedly by a smirking Ike Newton and—surprise of all surprises—an equally lewd Isaac Kennedy. Several times he called out her name and was awakened by his own shout.

Toward morning he broke out in a sweat and woke up with a violent case of the shivers. Feeding the flames, he moved closer and let the warmth seep into his pores. Drowsiness descended again and he dozed off, fitfully stirring every now and then to glance around.

Another dream terrified him beyond belief. In it, he saw Winona tied to a burning stake while prancing Utes whooped in delight around her. Gratefully, his mind then sank into an inky realm devoid of thoughts and dreams and he slumbered quietly, oblivious to the world around him.

The neighing of the horses awoke Nate with a start and he sat up to see the sun already above the eastern horizon. Furious at himself for oversleeping, he glanced toward the trees where the animals were tied and felt the short hairs at the nape of his neck tingle.

Standing twenty feet away, its eyes fixed balefully on the mounts, was an enormous grizzly.

Nate leaped to his feet, the Kentucky in his hands. No matter how many times he saw the brutes or tangled with them, he still couldn't get over their immense size and power.

The lords of the Rockies were awe-inspiring beasts. Standing four and a half feet high at the front shoulders when on all fours, their bulk was accented by the prominent bulge between their shoulder blades. With a length of over seven feet, grizzly bears were the undisputed masters of their domain. Not even the formidable wolverine could match a grizzly in combat. Whites and Indians alike feared them and gave them a wide berth whenever possible.

Now, as the grizzly swung its massive head to stare at Nate, his previous encounters with the fierce beasts flashed before him. The first time was when he was en route to the Rockies with his Uncle Zeke. At the Republican River a grizzly had charged him, and only by the grace of God had he survived. Weeks later, on the way to the rendezvous, another one had attacked him. Finally, while trapping beaver with Shakespeare, a third grizzly had charged him with the combined ferocity of all three.

He curled his thumb around the hammer and hoped this time would be different. Shakespeare had advised him to always stand completely still when confronted by a grizzly. Any movement might draw the mighty beast closer, and running was an engraved invitation to attack. So he stood his ground and waited for the bear to make the next move.

Nate knew that many mountaineers believed that no wild animal, no matter how savage, would dare attack the face of man. That was why most trappers, when charged by a grizzly, stood and faced the onrushing bruin with their gun at the ready. Nine times out of ten the tactic worked, the charging grizzly halting within yards of the human, only to wheel and race off. But there was always that tenth time when the grizzly didn't stop, and then the bear made short work of the trapper even if wounded first.

But Nate held little stock in this theory.

None other than Meriweather Lewis, of Lewis and Clark fame, had described the grizzly bear as extremely hard to die and the most fierce of all the wild creatures in existence. In *THE HISTORY OF THE EXPEDITION OF CAPTAINS LEWIS AND CLARK*, published in 1814, numerous spine-tingling encounters with grizzly bears were related.

The grizzly watching Nate suddenly advanced straight toward him. He held his breath, bracing for an attack, wondering if he might be able to reach the forest and clamber up a tree before being mauled to death.

Grunting, the bear halted. It cocked its head and regarded the buckskin-clad figure intently, as if trying to determine whether the man was edible.

For his part, Nate suppressed the stark terror that threatened to engulf him. He could see the bear's sides heaving as it breathed, see the brute's nose flaring as it sniffed the air for his scent. His mouth went dry and he nearly bolted.

The grizzly bear glanced at the horses for a moment, then nonchalantly turned and went into the woods, making little noise despite its bulk. Seconds later the shaggy beast was swallowed up by the forest.

Nate waited, scanning the perimeter of the clearing, dreading that the bear would circle around and come at him from another direction. After a minute he realized the grizzly had indeed departed and exhaled, only then realizing he had been holding his breath.

He walked to the horses and comforted them. Since the sun had already risen, he opted to forego breakfast and instead saddled Lambert's horse. He put out the fire by dumping a mound of snow on the flickering embers, took a long draught of ice-cold water from the stream, and mounted up.

Eager to reach Winona, Nate pushed the horses

hard, sticking to the tell-tale trail made by her abductors and their animals. His body still ached and his head still hurt, but the pain had diminished considerably. Of more concern was the bright snow. He didn't want a repeat of yesterday so he avoided staring directly at the shimmering cover when possible. By constantly looking down at the horse, then only briefly surveying the terrain ahead, he found that the glare didn't bother his eyes nearly as much as before.

He had to estimate the miles he covered. Two. Three. Five. There was still no sign of where Newton and company had camped for the night.

And then he saw the buzzards.

There were seven of the big black birds in all, swinging in wide, lazy circles hundreds of feet above the ground perhaps a quarter of a mile to the west. Their wings outspread, they soared on the uplifting air currents, their attention focused on something below.

Puzzled and not a little anxious, Nate urged his mount to go faster through the deep snow while hauling on the lead to pull the Indian stallion along. When at last he glimpsed a clearing, he slowed and held the Kentucky ready to fire. There were buzzards near the center, four of five of them clustered around a body lying in the snow.

What if it was Winona?

The unthinkable spurred Nate to lash his horse into a gallop. He burst from the trees in a spray of snow. Immediately the buzzards took to the air, noisily flapping their powerful wings, gaining altitude rapidly. He rode over to the corpse and reined up, elated to discover it was a man lying there, not a woman. Sliding down, he crouched and inspected the body.

Logic told Nate the dead man must be Ike Newton. The figure was the same size and wearing the same clothes the rogue mountaineer had worn when last Nate saw him. But identifying the man by his facial features was out of the question, simply because the face no longer existed. Judging from the powder burns on the shreds of forehead and chin remaining, the scoundrel had been shot in the face at a range of less than an inch. Then the buzzards had feasted on the exposed portions of Newton's body, pecking away at the fingers and consuming both eyes, the nose, and the soft areas of the mouth and cheeks. Between the ball and the birds there wasn't anything left but a few pieces of pinkish flesh and exposed bone.

The sight made Nate feel queasy. He stood and stepped away to catch his breath, glad that another foe had fallen but at a loss to explain the reason. Obviously the single shot he'd heard the night before had been the one that killed Newton. But who pulled the trigger? Isaac Kennedy? He grinned at the ludicrous notion. The storekeeper couldn't harm a fly, let alone kill in cold blood.

But if Kennedy hadn't committed the deed, then who? Certainly not Winona. Had she succeeded in slaying Newton, she would have headed in haste toward the cabin and he would have met her on the trail. Could it have been Indians, then? If so, the Utes were the likeliest candidates. And if his supposition was correct, it meant the Utes now had his wife and Kennedy and were taking them to a village.

He scanned the clearing, seeking signs of the Indians. If the Utes did attack the camp, there were bound to be plenty of tracks to confirm it. He saw where the string of horses had been tethered and the footprints of Newton, Kennedy, and Winona in the snow, but no others. Confused, he looked at the line of trees beyond where the pack animals had been tied and saw a sight that made him stiffen and his mouth go slack in utter bewilderment.

Chapter Fifteen

Isaac Kennedy was ready to keel over. He'd never felt so tired in all his life. It took tremendous effort to stay upright in the saddle, the Kentucky cradled in his right arm, and his eyes on the Shoshone woman riding a few feet in front of him. He yawned and glanced over his shoulder at the pack of horses he was leading, watching them plod wearily along.

Perhaps he'd made a mistake in traveling at night. Not only didn't they find Two Owls' village, but now all of them, including the animals, were exhausted. Having to contend with the cold and forging through the deep snow had taken a heavy toll.

They were nearing a point where the valley temporarily narrowed, with high hills to both the right and left. On their right the stream bubbled and gurgled over a stretch of rocks.

"Winona," Kennedy said.

She responded without looking at him. "Yes?"

"I figure we should take a break. What do you think?"

"You have the gun."

Kennedy hefted the rifle, his forehead creasing. "So? What are you trying to say?"

"You have the gun," Winona reiterated. "The decision is yours."

"But I want your opinion. What do you think we should do?"

"I think you should go back to the white man's land as fast as your horse will carry you. And I think you should let me go to find my husband."

"I'm not giving up now, not when I'm so close." Kennedy declared. "As far as your husband is concerned, you'll see him after we conclude our business with Two Owls."

"What business is that?"

"You'll know soon enough."

They rode on in a strained silence. Kennedy wished there was something he could say to dispell her resentment toward him. He sensed she despised his very presence. But her attitude would change once he took her back to the States. Once she became dependent on him for her well being and grew to appreciate the value of a dollar, she'd change her tune. Or, in this case, thirty thousand dollars. The thought made him chuckle.

Kennedy gazed to the south and saw several elk moving in the trees. He toyed with the notion of trying to shoot one, but since Winona would undoubtedly take off the second he squeezed the trigger and he would no longer have a loaded gun to keep her in line, he refrained. Besides, he knew he was a lousy shot and might well waste the ball.

Sighing, Kennedy let his eyes rove over the hills. To his joy, on the hill to the north, in a clearing halfway up, were seven mounted Indians who were watching Winona and him intently. Grinning, he reined up and waved.

The warriors simply stared.

"Winona," Kennedy said excitedly. "Look! Utes!"

She halted, turning her horse sideways. Gazing in the direction he was, she saw the seven men, her grip on her reins tightening. "We are in trouble."

"Why? Two Owls' warriors won't hurt us."

"Those men are not Utes."

"Which tribe are they from?" Kennedy inquired, amused by her nervousness. He felt confident he could talk his way out of any difficulty. If not, he could scare the seven off with a shot; surely the Indians weren't about to go up against a white man armed with a rifle since none of the band carried a gun.

"Those are Arapahos," Winona disclosed. "They live on the plains east of the mountains."

"What are they doing here?"

"Either they are hunting or on a raid," Winona speculated. "The Utes and the Arapahos fight all the time. We must take cover right away."

"And let them think we're afraid? Nonsense," Kennedy stated emphatically.

The seven warriors rode into the woods bordering the clearing, heading toward the valley floor.

Winona looked at the storekeeper, her expression grave. "Listen to me. We must run and find some-where we can defend ourselves or soon you will lose your hair and I will be on my way to an Arapaho village."

The earnest appeal impressed Kennedy. She rarely displayed any emotion, yet here she was genuinely frightened. Undoubtedly she didn't fully appreciate the change that had taken place inside him. Now that he could stand on his own feet, now that he had proven his manhood by slaying Ike Newton, he could protect her from anyone and anything. Still, to humor her, he nodded and said, "All right. Lead the way."

She expertly spun her horse and took off into the woods to the south, her hair flying, her robe flapping.

Tugging on the pack string lead, Kennedy followed. He was afraid she might try to pull far ahead and lose him. A check back failed to disclose the exact whereabouts of the seven warriors. They could be anywhere, approaching from any direction. He goaded his mount to go faster.

Winona made for the base of the southern hill. When she reached it, she turned to the left.

"Hold up!" Kennedy commanded, stopping. "You're going the wrong way. We want to go west, not east."

Halting abruptly, Winona swung toward him, her annoyance obvious. "If we go west the Arapahos will catch us easily."

"West is where Two Owls' village lies," Kennedy noted. "Are you trying to pull the wool over my eyes? Going east will only take us back toward your cabin." He jabbed a finger westward. "We go that way. Head out."

Hesitating, Winona gazed in the direction she wanted to go, then toward the hill the Arapahos were descending.

"I won't take no for an answer," Kennedy warned her, hefting the Kentucky rifle.

"You are a fool," Winona snapped, and reined her horse around. She rode past him without another glance, staying close to the slope.

Chuckling to himself, Kennedy trailed her. His newfound resolve amazed even him. To think that he had wasted so many years being a mouse when deep down he was a veritable tiger. For the very first time in his life he felt in control; he was the master of his own destiny instead of the slave of circumstances.

They rode for almost ten minutes without mishap, leaving both hills behind. All around them the forest lay deathly still. Even the birds had ceased to chirp.

Kennedy noticed the lack of wildlife and the quiet but attached no special significance to either. He noticed Winona constantly scanning the woods and grinned at her anxiety. As he had expected, those Arapahos hadn't given chase. He recalled all the gory tales Newton and Lambert had told him about Indians in general and was astonished at how gullible he'd been. Those illiterate trappers had exaggerated their stories, embellishing the yarns with outlandish claims of rampant Indian savagery. Well, now he knew better. Now he knew that he didn't have anything to be worried about so long as he kept his wits about him and didn't give in to mindless fear.

They passed through a stand of saplings, crossed a clearing, and entered a tract of tall pines.

Kennedy let his eyes dwell on the Shoshone's back. He tried to imagine her naked and tingled at the thought of lying abed with her. How unfortunate that she was heavy with child. He'd have to wait until after she delivered before he could—

Something streaked out of the vegetation on the right and thudded into the storekeeper's right calf.

Startled, lanced with pain, Kennedy glanced down and was stunned to behold the feathered end of an arrow jutting from his leg. Suddenly his horse whinnied and tried to buck him. He realized the arrow point and several inches of the thin shaft were imbedded in the animal's flesh. Clasping the reins firmly, he brought the horse under control. Only then did he look up and see Winona riding as fast as she could away from him.

"Wait!" Kennedy cried, and goaded his horse onward, retaining his grip on the string lead. The pain, surprisingly, subsided, although blood poured from the wound. He functioned mechanically, his mind unable to come to terms with the reality of being shot with an arrow. Glancing over his shoulder, he saw no sign of the war party.

With his right leg pinned to his mount's side, riding was awkward. Kennedy tried to wrench his leg loose, but couldn't. He heard a swishing sound and felt a sharp twinge in his lower left side. Peering down, he discovered the bloody tip of an arrow protruding from his abdomen.

He'd been hit again! Shot in the back, no less!

Kennedy rode harder. He didn't understand why there wasn't more pain. He'd never liked pain much and trembled at the idea of suffering intense agony. Skirting a pine, he tugged on the rope lead, listening to the muffled drumming of the many hooves to his rear. If he released the rope he could ride as fast as Winona. But doing so meant abandoning the pack animals, meant leaving the crates for the Arapahos. And he'd rather die than give up the merchandise that would bring him thirty thousand dollars or more.

A hammer seemed to strike him between the shoulder blades and his body was knocked forward over the saddle by the impact. Straightening, an odd burning sensation in his chest, Kennedy gasped at finding another crimson coated arrow tip and two inches of wooden shaft sticking from his torso.

They were skewering him at will!

He twisted, extended the Kentucky backwards, and, using just his right hand, fired. The shot had two consequences that took him unawares. First the recoil wrenched the rifle from his grip and it fell into the snow. Then the lead pack animals, frightened by the blast, the spurt of flame, and the cloud of gunpowder, went into a panicked frenzy, pulling at the lead rope in an effort to break free.

Kennedy lost his hold on the lead. He went ten more yards before he could bring the horse to a stop.

If he could retrieve the rifle, he still stood a chance. Starting to wheel his mount, he experienced a searing spasm in his left shoulder. Don't look! his mind screamed. It's just another arrow.

He brought the horse around and saw the pack animals merely standing there eight feet away, docile now. But where was the rifle? Retracing his steps, he spied the rifle stock poking out of the snow. All he had to do was reach it and he'd be fine. Dizziness hit him then, causing him to sway, and he thought for a second that he might pass out. A forceful blow hit him in the chest, then another, rocking him backwards. His vision cleared and he gaped in horror at two more arrows stuck in him.

No! This couldn't be happening!

His arms went weak and limp. A heartbeat later his legs did the same. Before he could straighten up, he fell to the right, toppling into the snow and tearing his impaled leg from the horse in the bargain. He crashed onto his right shoulder, the snow cushioning his descent.

Kennedy blinked and tried to rise. His body refused to cooperate. It occurred to him that he might be dying. Strangely, he felt no fear.

A shadow fell across him. Then another. Straining, he twisted his neck and saw a pair of buckskin clad Indians regarding him coldly. Others appeared beside them and they conversed in soft tones.

Kennedy groaned when one of the warriors stepped up and flipped him onto his back. He tried to speak, to tell them he was friendly, that he meant no harm, but his lips barely moved.

The Arapaho who had flipped him over drew a large knife from a beaded sheath on his left hip and squatted.

They were fixing to scalp him! Kennedy knew it and he braced himself for the ordeal. To his bewilderment, the warrior lowered the knife below his chin, not toward the top of his head. A peculiar stinging in his neck made him flinch. On its heels came the oddest feeling of all, as if warm water was spraying onto his throat.

The warrior raised the knife into view. Blood dripped from the keen blade.

Kennedy's pulse pounded in his temples. That was *his* blood! The savage had slit his throat. Tears filled his eyes and he could barely see the Indians move over to the pack animals. A crate smashed to the ground.

Loud, excited whoops burst from the warriors.

Tears poured down Kennedy's cheeks. The bastards had found the rifles! Now he would never be able to trade with Two Owls for all the beaver hides the Utes had caught during the past year. Now he would never reap the profit of his trip west. All that trouble, all that work, and for nothing. He should have stuck to storekeeping and told Ike Newton to go jump in a lake.

He took some small comfort from knowing Winona had eluded the war party. Hopefully, she would make it safely back to her husband. If anyone could protect her, it would be that fellow Grizzly Killer.

Another shadow hovered over him.

Kennedy peered upward. There stood the Indian who had slit his throat. He wanted to rise, to flail away, but could do nothing except watch in fascination as the warrior now produced a tomahawk. The Arapaho grinned at him, waved the tomahawk in the air, then raised it up high.

A pervailing calm had seeped into every fiber of Isaac Kennedy's being. With incredible clarity he observed the gleaming tomahawk streak straight at his face. There was a second of fleeting pain and one eye seemed to be sliding to the right while the other slid to the left. Then everything faded to black.

Chapter Sixteen

Nate ran to the trees and halted in front of a pine, not quite able to believe his eyes. There, propped against the trunk, was his Hawken. He scooped the rifle up, afraid it had been damaged somehow and that was the reason it had been left behind. To his amazement, the rifle was in perfect working order, the stock, barrel, and trigger mechanism intact. Confused, he walked to the horses.

None of this made any sense. Had Utes been responsible for slaying Ike Newton and taking Winona and the storekeeper, they would surely have taken the Hawken as well. Even if Indians weren't to blame—which he thought unlikely—no one in their right mind would ride off and leave an excellent Hawken rifle in the middle of nowhere.

No, it was as if someone had deliberately left the

Hawken there for him to find. But who? Certainly not
Newton, who lay there dead. Kennedy, perhaps. The
storekeeper had seemed to be the sort who would
help others in need. Or could his wife have done it?
Not very likely. He couldn't see any of the scoundrels
letting her get her hands on a gun.

Not about to look a gift horse in the mouth, Nate
reloaded his prized rifle, then slid the Kentucky into
a scabbard on Lambert's horse. With two rifles, the
flintlock, his tomahawk and knife at his disposal, he
felt ready to take on the entire Ute nation, if need be,
to rescue Winona.

Nate mounted and resumed his search. He gazed
skyward and saw the buzzards still circling. The big
birds would make short work of Ike Newton's remains. Between them and the varmints, in a day or
two all that remained of Newton would be bleached
bones.

He stayed with the tracks, pushing the horses,
eager to close the gap. Then, from far ahead, came
the distinct crack of a single shot. He reined in,
listening, waiting for more. When none sounded, he
lashed his mount into a gallop. So far luck had been
on his side. As far as he knew, Winona was still alive.
But the longer he took to reach her, the greater the
likelihood he would find her dead.

Winona raced for a quarter of a mile before she
saw signs of pursuit. Two Arapahos on sturdy, fleet
horses were hot on her trail. They spied her and
whooped in delight.

She grit her teeth and fled ever westward, desperately seeking a means of outsmarting the duo and
escaping. The mantle of snow would thwart any
attempt she made to conceal her tracks. Unless she
could outrun them, a slim chance given that her
horse was fatigued already, she would fall into their
clutches.

In one respect she was grateful. Had the war party been composed of Kiowas or Comanches, her life would be in immediate danger; both frequently killed female captives. Arapahos, on the other hand, weren't quite as bloodthirsty and often adopted females taken in raids into their tribes. Not that living as a prisoner of the Arapahos was in itself appealing.

She wanted her Nate, wanted to see his handsome face again and hold his powerful body in her arms. He must be out of his mind with worry for her and it was all her fault. She should have checked out the window before heading outside to feed the horses. At the very least she should have taken a flintlock. If she'd had a pistol in her hand when she opened the door and saw that man pointing a rifle at her, she could have tried to shoot him. Even if she'd failed, the delay would have given Nate time to bring his weapons to bear.

Yes, she had failed her husband and she felt mightily shamed by it. Shoshone women prided themselves on being good wives. A woman who couldn't keep her lodge clean and tidy, or couldn't cook or sew or prepare hides, or who failed to anticipate her husband's needs and give him the support he needed, was regarded as a failure in Shoshone society. She would be cast out by the other women and refused membership into the various womens' societies devoted to excellence in those arts and crafts so crucial to the happiness and welfare of any family. And although Shoshone women seldom went on raids, they were expected to aid in the defense of the village and to be there when their husbands needed them.

Nate had told her conditions were quite different among the whites. Many white women no longer bothered with those responsibilities that were common expressions of a Shoshone woman's love for her family, the cleaning and washing and sewing. They hired other women to do those chores and devoted

themselves to sitting around and chatting or buying
new clothes or taking strolls to get 'fresh air'. She
couldn't conceive of any woman spending time in
such a frivolous fashion, but then the ways of the
whites often mystified her. As a race they had lost
touch with the Great Medicine and were no longer
guided by the spirit in all things. They were too
interested in things going on outside them and not
enough in their inner being.

She looked back to discover the Arapahos had
gained hundreds of yards. Both men were grinning.
To them catching an unarmed woman constituted a
pleasant game. She wished she had a gun, or a bow or
a knife. She would teach them that Shoshone women
were not to be taken lightly.

The chase took them over a rise and ever farther
into the valley. Deer took flight at their approach. A
hawk observed the proceeding from far overhead.
Rabbits bounded into the brush.

Winona's horse began to flag. She felt equally
weary. Since her abduction she had been unable to
catch more than snatches of sleep. Her appetite had
diminished, and in her condition she needed to eat
for two. Traveling all night had further weakened her.
But she refused to give up. She would resist the
Arapahos until she collapsed from fatigue.

Suddenly nature itself conspired against her. In
front of her loomed a steep hillock slick with snow. If
she tried to go around she would lose much ground
so she went straight up. Her horse managed to go a
dozen feet before its hooves started slipping and
sliding.

Winona felt the animal going down. Fearful of the
consequences to the baby should the horse roll over
her, she threw herself to the right onto her shoulder.
The heavy buffalo robe absorbed the brunt of the
plunge and she rolled upright. Her horse was on its

side, sliding down to the bottom of the hillock, plowing a wide path through the snow.

She forged through the clinging white blanket and reached the animal as it went to stand. Speaking softly, she grabbed the bridle and tried to soothe its jangled nerves. Brittle laughter brought her around to confront its source.

Thirty feet out, riding slowly, were the two Arapahos. They joked and laughed, pointing at her horse and the slope.

Winona went to swing on her mount, but a sharp pain in her belly made her double over and gasp. She must be careful or she would hurt the baby. The possibility of losing the child filled her with dread. Struggling to keep her composure, she straightened and faced the Arapahos.

Both were rugged examples of their tribe, hardened by a life that brooked no flabbiness or laziness. They wore buckskins styled in the manner of their people. One wore his hair long and flowing, the other wore his braided. They both carried bows and sported full quivers on their backs.

Grinning, the warriors rode closer and halted. The man with the braided hair addressed her in his own tongue.

Winona stood impassively. She knew few words in the Arapaho language and refused to respond in sign. Then she received a shock.

"What is a Shoshone woman doing so far from her tribe?" the braided one asked in perfect Shoshone.

Instead of answering, Winona rejoined sarcastically, "Where did an Arapaho dog learn to speak the language of those who are his betters?"

The warrior laughed uproariously. He translated for the other man and they both regarded her with commingled amusement and respect.

"I am He Wolf," the braided warrior announced. "I

once had a Shoshone wife for several winters after I took her in a raid. She taught me your tongue, but otherwise she was useless. She could not cook and her feet were cold at night. I traded her for three horses." He pointed at his companion. "This is Swift Wind In The Morning. How are you called?"

"Winona."

"And what were you doing with that fat white man?"

"He stole me from my lodge, which is only a few sleeps from here. Soon my husband will come to take me back."

He Wolf translated again. Swift Wind In The Morning shifted and began to scan the surrounding woods carefully.

"You lie, woman," He Wolf declared. "There are no Shoshone lodges in this part of the mountains."

Winona allowed herself the luxury of a smirk. "I did not say it was a Shoshone lodge. My husband is a white man and we live in a house of wood. He is as strong as three men and does not know the meaning of fear. You would be wise to let me go to him before he finds you and feeds you to the buzzard and bear."

"How is this great warrior called?" He Wolf inquired sarcastically.

"He is known as Grizzly Killer."

He Wolf's eyes narrowed. "I have heard of such a white from our brothers, the Cheyennes. They say this man killed a grizzly using just a knife."

"He has killed three grizzlies," Winona boasted proudly, "and ten times that many enemies. Soon he will add your hair to the list."

After mulling her words for a bit, He Wolf turned to Swift Wind In The Morning and the two conversed in their own language. Finally He Wolf stared at her again.

"We are taking you with us. Get on your horse."

"You will not live to regret this," Winona assured him.

"There are seven of us on this raid. We are more than a match for any ten white men, let alone one," He Wolf asserted, and jerked his thumb at her animal. "Now climb on your horse."

Since there was no other choice, Winona complied, her buffalo robe falling open as she did. The pain in her abdomen had abated and she felt well enough to ride.

He Wolf leaned forward, studying her figure as she settled on the animal. "You are with child," he stated in surprise. "How many moons until the baby will be born?"

"Three."

"This is bad news," He Wolf said. "We do not want a half-breed in our village."

"My son will be a great man like his father. He will honor any tribe who befriends him."

"How do you know it is a boy?"

"I know."

Grunting, He Wolf motioned for her to precede them.

Despite Winona's display of courage and her confidence in Nate, she was extremely worried. The Arapaho warrior had a point. They were seven; Nate but one. The odds were overwhelmingly in their favor. She must find a way to aid her husband. Outsmarting those two wicked trappers and the lecher Kennedy had been relatively easy; she'd been able to hide Nate's knife and tomahawk under their bed without being detected, and later had left the Hawken propped against a tree for Nate instead of putting it on the pack animals as Kennedy had ordered. But tricking the Arapahos would not be so easy. They were naturally more alert than the white men had been, and one of them was bound to be watching every move she made. Still, as Nate's partner for life she couldn't sit idly by and do nothing. A good wife always stood by her husband's side no matter the odds.

They rode back to the pack animals.

Winona saw Isaac Kennedy lying dead in crimson stained snow, his face split wide open. The five other warriors were laughing and joking, standing near a crate that had broken apart, each man holding in his hands one of the items that had been packed inside.

Rifles!

Startled, Winona gazed at the other crates. From the comments the trappers and Kennedy had made, she now understood everything. When Newton and Lambert had been captured by Two Owls a year ago, they must have promised to bring the Ute chief guns in exchange for their lives. No doubt they had offered to trade the firearms for prime beaver pelts and other furs. But now dozens of top quality rifles were in the possession of the Arapahos, who would not hesitate to use them against other tribes and whites alike if need be.

She knew that rifles were formidable weapons. The more powerful guns could shoot farther than bows and in the hands of skilled shooters, such as Nate, they were amazingly accurate and reliable. Already she knew of instances where badly outnumbered trappers had held off determined attacking warriors using the lethal firepower of their rifles.

Most of the guns owned by Indians were inferior to those employed by the whites. Fusees, those cheap trade rifles frequently bestowed on unsuspecting warriors, had neither the range nor the accuracy of Kentucky rifles and Hawkens. Consequently, the possession of guns had not made any difference so far in deciding the outcome of the many raids and encounters between various tribes. But all that could change, she realized. If the Arapahos learned to use the rifles in those crates, they might well be able to conquer all their foes and become the dominant tribe west of the Great River.

The warriors prepared to depart. He Wolf and Swift Wind In The Morning also claimed rifles, and the rest from the broken crate were tied in a bundle on a pack horse. As the men worked they glanced repeatedly at the surrounding forest.

Winona knew they were looking for Utes. The shot fired earlier would attract any Ute warriors in the vicinity. And since this was Ute territory, the Arapahos could find themselves overwhelmed by the fierce mountain dwellers.

Soon they were on their way, bearing to the northeast. They crossed the stream and made for the hills bordering the valley. Forced to ride between He Wolf and Swift Wind in the Morning, Winona resigned herself to going along with them for the time being. She only hoped she could escape before Nate overtook the band or there would be much blood spilled —and some of it might be his.

Chapter Seventeen

Nate sat astride Lambert's horse and stared down at the grisly remains of Isaac Kennedy. Jagged flesh and a portion of the cranium had been exposed by a tomahawk blow to the head. Congealed blood coated the man's chin and neck. The buzzards had yet to discover the body and none of the carrion eaters had touched it. He felt a twinge of regret that the kindly storekeeper had been killed. The man should never have ventured into the Rocky Mountains. Kennedy had been as out of place in the wilderness as he would be now back in the city.

Turning the horse, Nate examined the snow, discovering the tracks of many Indians, as well as those of the pack animals, and the trail they'd made heading to the northeast. As near as he could tell, Kennedy and Winona had been alone when they were ambushed by warriors. He saw where a single horse had ridden on west at great speed, and then three horses had returned. By the depth of the hooves he knew all three carried riders and surmised one of them had been his darling wife. He wasn't skilled enough to tell if the footprints scattered about had been made by Utes or warriors from another tribe, but the direction of travel hinted that he wasn't dealing with Two Owls' people.

He squared his broad shoulders and rode out, squinting up at the sun. If he pushed himself he might overtake the band by nightfall. He estimated there were at least a half-dozen warriors in the war party, enough to give any sane man pause. But short of death, he wasn't about to stop.

The gleaming snow bothered his eyes again, compelling him to avert his gaze from the brilliant crust as much as possible. He was hungry and thirsty but ignored both sensations. There would be time to eat *after* Winona was safe in his arms, not before.

The trail brought him to the hills on the north side of the valley. The band had skirted the base of one, passed between it and the next hill, then turned to the east, staying in a narrow tract between the hills and a high range of mountains rearing up to the clouds.

He became convinced that the band didn't consist of Utes. Whoever these warriors were, they were trying to keep out of sight by taking the route between the foothills and the mountains, a tactic only warriors belonging to a tribe at war with the Utes would use. He mentally ticked off a list of likely candidates. There were the feared Blackfeet, the Bloods, the Crows, the Cheyennes, the Arapahos, or possibly the Kiowas or Comanches. He wouldn't know until he saw them, and even then he might not be able to identify the band because he hadn't previously encountered members from all of those tribes.

All he could do was ride and pray.

The golden orb in the azure sky arced ever higher and he drew abreast of a narrow gap in the mountains. The tracks went right into it. Stopping, he studied the opening, his suspicions aroused. Only twenty feet wide and winding in serpentine fashion, the gap was a perfect spot for an ambush. The slopes on both sides were covered with snow laden trees. There could be warriors concealed there at that very moment, watching his every move.

He hesitated, torn between common sense and devotion to Winona. To go around the gap would take him hours. Since time was of the essence, he rested the Hawken across his pommel and rode on, a swarm of butterflies fluttering in his stomach. He searched the snow for telltale tracks leading into the trees. To his surprise, there were none.

At the north end of the gap he halted once more. Before him stretched a 'hole', as most trappers and mountaineers would call it, a level valley averaging five miles in width and completely hemmed in by mountains. The trail went straight across the open ground into woods a hundred yards off.

Evidently the war party had no idea anyone was following them. He nodded in satisfaction and moved out, firmly gripping the lead rope to Barking Dog's horse. Lambert's animal diligently forged through the deep snow, cold breath puffing from its nostrils.

Somewhere a bird screeched.

Nate scanned the treeline, not really expecting trouble. Any ambush would have been sprung in the gap—or so he believed until he registered movement in the shadows. A second later a pair of mounted warriors appeared, each armed with a bow and arrow. At once they voiced their war cries and charged.

When Winona saw the two Arapahos drop back from the column she immediately knew their purpose and unconsciously halted, her anxiety over Nate's welfare eclipsing her prudence.

"Keep going," He Wolf instructed gruffly. He was on her right and had reined in when she did.

Reluctantly Winona complied, her heart pounding in her chest. Those men would wait for Nate and attack him as soon as he showed up. She licked her lips, debating whether to bolt into the trees in an effort to escape. Only the knowledge that the Arapahos would easily catch her dissuaded her from making the attempt. That, and her concern for the new life in her body. More strenuous riding might well cause her to deliver prematurely, a fate she would avoid at all costs. The baby hadn't been born yet but already it was a part of Nate and her, as important to them as their own lives. This was a fulfillment of their cherished dreams and an investment in the future of their bloodline, a full-fledged member of the family to be carefully nurtured every moment.

She had noticed that the two warriors staying behind took only bows and arrows. As near as she could determine, although the Arapahos were tremendously excited over discovering the guns there wasn't a one of them who had ever fired a rifle and knew how to properly load the black powder and a ball. No doubt they would learn in time. But for now they couldn't make use of the devastating firepower the dozens of rifles held against Nate, which relieved her greatly.

She rode in tense anticipation of hearing gunshots, paying no attention to her captors until He Wolf addressed her.

"You are worried about your precious Grizzly Killer," he commented sarcastically.

"No," Winona lied.

"If he is all you claimed, you would have nothing to worry about," He Wolf mocked her. "His reputation is probably highly overrated. After all, he is only a white man."

"But he has learned to live like us and to like our ways," Winona told him. "He is not like most whites. He does not look down on us."

"All whites should be rubbed out," the Arapaho stated emphatically. "They are not worth the air they breathe."

"Why do you hate them so?"

"Because they have no respect for the spirits," He Wolf declared. "Most of them care about nothing except furs and money. They know nothing of the Great Medicine, nothing of the spirit in all things. They come to our land, kill the beaver and the buffalo, and act like they are better than us." He snorted. "I say wipe them all out."

"The whites will never go away," Winona said. "From what my husband tells me, there are more whites than there are rocks in these mountains, more even than all the blades of grass on the plains."

He Wolf laughed. "Do you believe everything your husband tells you?"

"He does not lie."

"Bah! All whites speak with two tongues. None of them would know the truth if it bit them on the nose."

They rode in silence for a quarter of a mile.

"I would like to know something," He Wolf said. "You make me curious."

"About what?"

"You," He Wolf said. "You seem to be a proud Shoshone woman, yet you have taken a white man for a husband. Why? What do you see in him that you could not find in any Shoshone man?"

Winona glanced at the Arapaho, wondering if he was taunting her again. His expression convinced her of his sincerity. He truly wanted to know. "Men are men and women are women no matter the color of their skin and the ways of life they have known. Oh, there are differences, but deep down we are all people. The reason I took Grizzly Killer for my life partner is very simple. He makes my heart sing."

For a while He Wolf didn't speak, then he responded softly. "I envy you, Winona. My heart never sang for any woman, although my loins have hungered after several. One day, perhaps, I will know the joy of love."

"Not if you don't release me so I can return to my husband. He will kill every one of you if you do not."

"Your foolishness grates on my nerves," He Wolf remarked. "Do not expect any pity from me when your husband's scalp is hanging in one of our lodges and you are wailing your grief to the sky."

At that instant, from the direction of the gap, there arose loud yells. War whoops.

Winona reined up in alarm.

Grinning, He Wolf paused to look back. "Now we will have the test of your words. And soon I will hold Grizzly Killer's hair in my hands."

Nate stopped, released the lead, and whipped the Hawken to his right shoulder. Both warriors already had shafts nocked to their bow strings and were drawing those strings back, trying to hold the bows steady as they attacked, not an easy feat when galloping through heavy snow. He cocked the hammer, took a bead on the man on the right, held it several seconds to be sure, then squeezed the trigger.

The Hawken boomed at the selfsame moment the two warriors let their arrows fly.

Nate saw the man on the right throw his arms into the air and hurtle off the rear of his onrushing mount. Just then a pair of streaking shafts cleaved the air within inches of his head, one on either side. He

lowered the Hawken to the saddle and tugged on the
Kentucky, sliding the rifle from its scabbard. A
glance showed him the second warrior coming on
strong, another arrow nocked and ready.

The Indian loosed the shaft.

This time Nate wrenched his horse to the right, and
it was well he did so for the arrow whizzed through
the very space his head had occupied. He urged the
animal forward, elevating the Kentucky as he did,
electing to meet his foe head-on.

Exhibiting astonishing ability, the warrior had a
third shaft nocked and was taking certain aim.

Nate did likewise, struggling to keep the barrel
from bobbing up and down with the rhythm of his
horse. He rushed his shot to prevent the warrior from
getting too close, the Kentucky cracking loudly as he
stroked the trigger.

The ball took the man high in the left shoulder and
flipped him off his steed. He fell onto his right side in
the snow, the bow and arrow flying from his fingers.
But he was far from finished. Rolling to his feet, he
ignored the bleeding hole in his shoulder and produced a war club that he waved overhead as he ran
forward.

While admiring the man's courage, Nate knew he
couldn't allow the warrior to get within striking
range. Holding both rifles in the same hand he held
the reins, he yanked the flintlock from under his belt
and cocked the pistol while bearing down on his
adversary.

The warrior, now twenty yards off, whooped his
defiance.

Nate waited until only half that distance separated
them before firing. The heavy pistol blasted and
bucked his arm upward.

A hole blossomed in the Indian's forehead. He
seemed to slam into an invisible wall, his charge

checked in midstride. Slowly crumbling, he stumbled a few feet, his mouth moving soundlessly. Then he pitched onto his face with his arms out flung.

Reining up, Nate replaced the flintlock, drew his tomahawk, and slid to the ground. He stepped to the man's side and flipped him over to verify the warrior had been slain. Not that there could be much doubt. One look was all it took to confirm the Indian would never ambush another mountaineer.

Nate glanced at the first warrior he'd slain, who was prone and motionless, then devoted his energies to reloading all of his guns. As he worked, he replayed the attack in his mind. Why had the warriors confronted him head-on when they could easily have shot him from concealment? If they had waited until he was close to the trees, he would have fallen without getting off a shot. Surely they'd realized as much.

So why had they brazenly charged him in the open?

He recollected the stories his Uncle Zeke and Shakespeare had told him about Indian conflicts and recalled his own experiences. Many Indian tribes, he knew, relished warfare; the Blackfeet and the Comanches were just two examples of tribes existing in a perpetual state of war. But it was not the actual bloody fighting they relished so much as it was the chance to gain personal glory.

As a consequence of this urge, most tribes adhered to rules of conduct in warfare, rules designed to garner individual warriors the greatest possible honor. And while the rules varied slightly from tribe to tribe, they all revolved around the counting of *coup*.

The word came from a French term having to do with striking or hitting another. Warriors took great pride in engaging enemies face to face. Those who exposed themselves during a battle ranked higher than those who killed while hidden. Also, those who slew a foe using their hands, a tomahawk, a stick or a lance, were rated above those who killed from a distance using a bow or a gun.

Did that have something to do with the reason the two warriors charged him outright? Sure, they'd used bows, but probably only because they felt they had to in order to stand a fair chance against his rifles.

He gazed at the dead man near his moccasins, trying to identify the warrior's tribe of origin. The style of buckskins and the Indian's braided hair were indicative of the Cheyennes, but not quite the same. Zeke had once told him that the Arapahos and the Cheyennes were the closest of allies, and that Arapaho customs and attire strongly mimicked those of the Cheyennes. Was it possible, then, that he was up against a war party of Arapahos?

At length Nate finished reloading and remounted. He rode back to retrieve Barking Dog's stallion, which had halted the moment he released it, then headed for the forest with the Hawken clutched in his right hand. A brief pause beside the first warrior confirmed the man was dead.

Exercising supreme caution, Nate continued to the treeline. He saw no sign of more Arapahos. The rest must be farther ahead with Winona and the pack animals.

Advancing into the woods, he stopped long enough to loop the stallion's lead around a branch. He wanted his hands free when he caught up with the war party. As an added preparation, he rested the Kentucky across his thighs.

Believing himself as prepared as possible, Nate brought his horse to a steady trot. The tracks were as easy to follow as ever, and half a mile into the trees he spied fresh horse droppings in the snow, so fresh that the droppings had not yet had time to harden and freeze or be covered sinking in the snow. He realized he would overtake them soon. Girding himself, he kept on going, and as he did he thought of a psalm his mother had often read to him when he was a small child. How did it go again? Oh, yeah. He commenced quietly mouthing the words: "The Lord is my shepherd. . . ."

Chapter Eighteen

Unbridled terror overflowed Winona's heart at the sound of the first shot. Her mind filled with horrid images of Nate being transfixed by arrows. She couldn't have moved if her life depended on it, but fortunately none of the Arapahos were moving, either. They were as intently interested in the outcome of the battle as she was, each man sitting with his head cocked to listen better. He Wolf had swung his mount completely around and sat with a stern expression.

A second shot cracked, then there were more whoops, and finally a third gun discharged.

Silence ensued.

All of the Arapahos began talking at once and gesturing excitedly along their backtrail.

A twinge of relief contended with Winona's fear for

her husband's life. Nate had fired three times, indicating the two warriors hadn't taken him by surprise. And knowing how well he could shoot, she surmised there were now two less members of the war party.

He Wolf glanced at her, his countenance somber. "It seems your husband is worthy of his name."

"I told you," Winona gloated.

"He will catch us soon if he has not been wounded," He Wolf remarked, surveying the landscape ahead. "We must prepare."

"What will you do?"

"You know what we must do," He Wolf said. He shifted and barked instructions to the other warriors. Immediately they all moved on, riding swiftly, pulling the reluctant pack animals along, making for a meadow visible through the trees to the northeast.

Winona deliberately stayed alongside He Wolf. "You can let me go. I will persuade my husband to let you leave this territory in peace."

"The Arapahos are not cowards. We do not run from battle."

"All my husband wants is me," Winona said, then quickly corrected herself, "and our horses. You can take the guns back to your people. Think of what so many rifles would mean to your tribe."

"I do not need a woman to instruct me in matters that rightfully concern only warriors," He Wolf said indignantly. He looked at her sternly. "You are wasting your breath if you think you can talk us out of killing your husband. He has counted coup on us. Now we will count coup on him."

"You are a fool."

The Arapaho glared at her. "Am I? Stare into my eyes and tell me that a Shoshone warrior would do any differently than I am doing."

Winona frowned. "I cannot."

"No," He Wolf said. "I knew you could not deny the

truth. No warrior would simply ride off now. We must make a stand or we will not be able to hold our heads up again."

"Then I have a request to make."

"You are in no position to be making requests."

"Give me a weapon so I can fight by my husband's side."

The Arapaho looked at her. "You would do such a thing?"

"A wife must share her husband's fate."

The corner of He Wolf's mouth curled in a lopsided grin and his eyes radiated appreciation. "You are an extraordinary woman, Winona. After I have slain Grizzly Killer, I will give much thought to taking you for my wife."

Bestowing a sweet smile on him, Winona said, "I would rather be thrown off a cliff or fed to wolves."

A hearty laugh burst from He Wolf. "I would say this Grizzly Killer has met his match in you. Are all Shoshone women so filled with spirit?"

"I cannot speak for all women. I am as I am."

The war party came to the edge of the snow covered meadow, which encompassed a tract of some four acres. They headed toward the center, several warriors bringing up the rear with their eyes on the forest.

Barely able to contain her anxiety, Winona tried one last appeal. "Would you ride on as fast as you can and forget about fighting my husband if I agree to become your wife?"

He Wolf's astonishment showed as he gazed at her. "You love him that much?"

"Yes."

"No wonder he will stop at nothing to get you back," He Wolf said. "But you can save your words. We will not tuck our tails between our legs and slink away like scared dogs. We will meet him here and be done with it."

Winona fell silent. She had used every argument she could think of, to no avail. The battle was inevitable. Now she must think of a means to help Nate without getting herself killed, if possible. If not, then she would die as a Shoshone woman should die, giving her life so her husband might live.

The war party reached the middle of the meadow and halted. After a brief discussion the five Arapahos aligned themselves in a row, positioning themselves about ten yards apart, their mounts facing the forest where Nate would soon appear. He Wolf occupied the center post, directly in front of Winona and the pack animals.

She stared at the warrior's back, her mind in turmoil. Perhaps, if she darted in front of the Arapahos when Nate appeared, it would so distract them that Nate would be able to shoot a couple of them before they could charge. Even so, there would be enough left to easily overpower him.

None of the Arapahos spoke, none displayed the slightest fear. They sat proudly, their spines rigid, ready to acquit themselves honorably. They each held a bow, an arrow nocked to the string.

Winona had never been so nervous. She scanned the treeline, eager to see Nate but dreading what would ensue. If anything happened to him, if he was killed, she wouldn't want to go on. In the time they had been together, sharing every aspect of their lives and an intimacy that touched the depths of her inner spirit, she had grown to care for him with an affection that eclipsed all else. It was an affection that surprised her in its intensity and depth of passion. She had never known love could be so profound, so exalting.

As a small girl playing in the Shoshone village she had often imagined what marriage would be like and pictured in her mind the man most likely to win her heart. Always had that fantasy figure been a handsome Shoshone warrior, a man who had counted more coup than all the rest of the tribe combined. Had anyone told her she would one day marry a white man, she would have laughed at their insanity.

Over the years many warriors had shown an interest in her. Quite a few had approached her father about taking her into their lodge, offering horses and robes and weapons, enough to make her father wealthy. Yet her wise father had never accepted any offer without first consulting her, and she'd always declined. Her mother had urged her to accept before she acquired a reputation as too hard to get, rightfully pointing out that some of her suitors were prominent men in the Shoshone nation and that any woman in her right mind would leap at the chance to marry them.

But Winona had remained aloof. Even she had been hard pressed to explain her behavior. She found many of the men attractive, but they failed to stir her heart. Why, she didn't know, until she saw Nathaniel King for the first time. It was as if a tiny barb had punctured her heart and let out all the love stored inside for years.

Somehow, in a mysterious manner she could not comprehend nor resist, she knew from the start that Nate would be the man she married. The knowledge came as automatically as the certainty that the sun would rise each morning and dark clouds from the west brought heavy rain.

Now she fidgeted and strained her eyes to pierce the shadows under the trees.

The time seemed to drag by.

Nothing moved in the woods.

Off to the east a lone hawk soared, seeking prey.

She began to wonder if Nate had been wounded by the other two warriors. Why else was he taking so long? Then she heard a sound that made her heart leap into her throat and she spun her horse around in amazement.

Nate was pushing ahead recklessly, anxious to catch the Arapahos, when he realized his mistake and abruptly reined up. It wouldn't do to blunder in among the war party like a greenhorn. As Shakespeare had often admonished him, those who survived the longest in the savage wilderness were those who used their heads in a crisis. Craftiness counted more in the issue of life and death than mere brawn. So to rescue Winona and come out alive he must become as crafty as an old fox.

He moved out again, only slower this time, peering intently at the forest before him. From the gait indicated by the tracks, he realized the war party had picked up the pace. He tried to outthink them, to anticipate their next move. What would he do if he was in their place? Set up another ambush, only this time do it right? Or find a spot to make a stand and finish the affray for good?

What was that?

Nate stopped again at spying a stretch of white ahead. He glimpsed movement. Holding a rifle in each hand, he slid to the ground and crouched behind a nearby tree. The distance was too great for him to distinguish details, but there appeared to be a number of riders in a field or a meadow beyond the trees. It took no genius to figure out who they were.

He bent at the waist and advanced until he could see clearly. At the sight of Winona he almost cried out her name in relief. He let his gaze linger on her for a minute before paying any attention to the members of the war party. There were five warriors all told, each one carrying bows.

A frown creased his mouth. Five to one were pathetic odds, all the more so since he couldn't hope to shoot all the Arapahos before one of them nailed him. Two, yes. Maybe three. Four if he was incredibly lucky. But never five.

He tried to come up with a plan, some way of defeating the warriors without endangering himself, but there simply wasn't a means of doing so. Oh, he could hide at the edge of the trees and shoot the warriors from concealment, in which case he stood a fair chance of slaying all five. But even then, they would see the smoke from his rifles and know exactly where to send their shafts. He discarded the idea, not because the gunsmoke would give him away, but because he wouldn't stoop so low as to shoot men from ambush. Only a coward would perform such a dastardly deed.

He returned to his horse, pondering furiously. Since he couldn't honorably shoot them from the relative safety of the forest, and since a frontal attack would leave him riddled with arrows, he came up with another way to go about tackling them. Swinging into the saddle, he placed the Kentucky in his lap and rode to the right. Staying far enough back from the meadow that the Indians couldn't possibly see him, he made a wide loop around them.

His plan was simple. He'd come up on the warriors from the rear. By the time they awoke to his presence, he might kill two or three. Then it would be a matter of overcoming the remainder with his knife and tomahawk.

He considered that he might well die but felt no fear. If Winona lived, the sacrifice was worth it. She had brought him the greatest happiness any man could ever know; his gratitude was boundless, his very existence in the palms of her hands. Now he could demonstrate the depth of his love, could repay her for her kindness and compassion. He regretted, though, that he might not live to see his son or daughter grow to adulthood. The notion of being a father greatly appealed to him.

His horse plodded along wearily, the thud of its hooves muffled by the snow. He checked his knife and tomahawk, making sure both weren't wedged too tightly under his belt. Then he rechecked the flint-lock, verifying the pistol was loaded.

By the time he arrived on the north side of the meadow he was beginning to feel edgy. He licked his lips and halted at the treeline. Neither the Arapahos nor Winona had moved.

Nate raised the Hawken, about to charge, then paused. If he shot those warriors in the back, it would be the same as shooting them from ambush. He might as well paint a yellow stripe down his back. No man worthy of his name would do such a thing.

He grinned at his foolishness, lowered the rifle, and rode from the forest, going slowly, amazed none of the Arapahos had awakened to his presence yet. Not even Winona, whose intuition was superb, had realized he was there. When only ten feet from the pack animals, he stopped, took a deep breath, and asked in a loud, clear voice: "Are you looking for someone?"

Chapter Nineteen

The startled expressions on the Arapahos as they wheeled their mounts struck Nate as so comical that he almost laughed. He had time for just a quick glance at Winona, whose face lit up with affection and hope, and then he concentrated on his five adversaries, all of whom were regarding him in commingled disbelief and fascination.

"You are Grizzly Killer," stated the warrior in the middle of the line, speaking in perfect Shoshone. "We have heard much about you."

"I have come for my wife and our horses," Nate said. "I have no wish to fight you unless you force it on me."

The warrior translated for the benefit of his companions. None of the others spoke. They were staring at Nate, at his guns.

Winona moved her horse over next to her husband's. The Arapahos made no move to interfere. She leaned toward him and said softly, "My heart is happy at seeing you again."

"As is mine," Nate replied.

She pointed at the crates. "They contain dozens of rifles and ammunition. Kennedy and the trappers planned to trade them to Two Owls for beaver furs."

Nate felt a sinking sensation in the pit of his stomach. Now there was no way he could simply ride off with Winona and let the matter drop. Those guns could be used to kill mountaineers. At the very least they would make the Arapahos the most powerful nation west of the Mississippi River, enabling them to conquer all the other tribes.

"I am He Wolf," the warrior who knew the Shoshone tongue declared. "We have heard that you are very brave."

"A man does what he must."

"True. And we must kill you," He Wolf said matter-of-factly. He extended his bow and smiled. "I see you have three guns. You might be able to shoot three of us before we slay you, but we will slay you in the end."

Nate didn't doubt it. He wondered where his own flintlocks were, the pair Newton and Lambert had taken from the cabin. Perhaps they were packed with the supplies or the rifles. If he had five guns, he just might prevail. But he didn't, and all the wishing in the world wouldn't help him one bit.

"It would be too easy for us to kill you with arrows," He Wolf was saying. "There is no honor in that, no challenge. I propose to fight you man on man, one at a time, so that the warrior who finally takes your hair can claim the highest coup. What do you say, Grizzly Killer?"

"None of you will use your bows and I'm not supposed to use my guns?"

"Those are the terms."

"I mean no insult, but how do I know I can trust you?" Nate responded.

He Wolf addressed his fellows and all five of them tossed their bows to the ground. The warrior pointed at the Hawken with one hand while drawing a knife with the other. "What about you, Grizzly Killer? Are you truly as brave as they say, or are the words told about you around campfires nothing but lies?"

For an answer Nate gave his rifles to Winona. She frowned as she took them. "If anything happens to me, ride off," he advised.

"If anything happens to you, I do not care if I live or die."

Nate slid the flintlock from under his belt and motioned for her to take the pistol. "You owe it to our unborn child to live. Promise me you will try if I die."

With evident reluctance Winona answered, "I will do as you want, husband. But the rest of my days will be spent in misery." She placed the flintlock in her lap, her shoulders slumping.

Suppressing an urge to take her into his arms, Nate drew his tomahawk and rode a dozen feet to the left. He eyed the Arapahos and hefted the weapon. "I am ready when you are, He Wolf. Prove to me that Arapaho warriors deserve to be called men."

"Even the Blackfeet fear us," He Wolf bragged, and spoke to his fellow tribesmen in his own tongue.

Suddenly the warrior on the far left of the line, the youngest of the bunch, vented a piercing whoop and charged, waving a war club overhead.

Nate wasn't about to sit there and let them bring the fight to him. To win he must take the offensive, must keep them off their guard. Consequently he goaded his horse into motion, galloping to meet his first adversary head-on, the tomahawk firmly clasped in his right hand. He bent low over the saddle, his gaze glued to the oncoming warrior's club.

The young Arapaho was too eager for his own good. He leaned out to the side, trying to increase his reach but exposing his torso in the process.

Hoping that Lambert's horse was well trained, Nate waited until he was only eight feet from the warrior before wrenching on the reins and cutting the animal sharply to the right. Almost simultaneously he reined up, stopping on the head of a pin, as it were. Unable to compensate, the young Arapaho lunged outward even further and swung his club. Nate knew the swing would miss before the warrior executed it. He whipped his body to the right, turning almost completely around in the saddle, using a backhand strike, and sank the gleaming edge of his tomahawk into the hapless Arapaho's neck as the man went racing past. The edge bit deep, severing veins and arteries, causing blood to spray like a fountain.

Swaying wildly, the warrior rode another ten yards before he pitched from his mount and landed face down in the snow. He tried to rise, his arms quivering, but collapsed in shock with his lifeblood spurting over the white blanket embracing his form.

Nate faced the rest of the band. They were staring grimly at their fallen companion. Spurned into action, the next warrior on the left shrieked and galloped to the attack, a tomahawk in his right hand, his features contorted in rage. Nate rode forward, keeping his own dripping tomahawk close to his side. This next warrior was older, more battle seasoned, and would be harder to dispatch. He girded his body for his next tactic, and when the two horses were almost abreast he swung to the off side, clinging to his animal with just his left leg and left arm.

The warrior cleaved the air as he went past, narrowly missing the exposed leg.

Drawing back on the reins as he straightened, Nate

turned his horse around and closed. The Arapaho was turning his stallion, or trying to, because his animal shied at the sight of Nate's horse bearing rapidly down. Struggling to get the stallion to obey, the warrior lifted his tomahawk in a defensive gesture.

Nate aimed a terrific swipe at the Arapaho's head, knowing full well the man would deflect it. Their weapons clashed and his slid off to the right. Almost in the same motion he reversed direction, lancing his tomahawk into the warrior's side a few inches below the ribs.

The Arapaho stiffened and gasped, then goaded the stallion to the right, losing all interest in the conflict. He clutched at the wound, his fingers becoming slick with blood.

Nate didn't bother to go after him. Instead he urged his horse straight toward He Wolf, his mouth set in a grim line. He couldn't afford to slack off a bit; he must keep attacking until he triumphed or died.

He Wolf was staring at the injured warrior. His gaze shifted to Nate and he smiled enigmatically. Then he lifted his knife and brought his own horse up to top speed, snow showering in all directions from its driving legs.

Nate had about used up his bag of tricks. If he was any judge of character, then He Wolf was a veteran of many encounters who wouldn't be fooled by clever horsemanship. He must do something totally unexpected, something that would take He Wolf completely unawares. Only one idea occurred to him and he mentally balked at trying it. Such madness could well result in his own death.

But what choice did he have?

He made as if to pass He Wolf on the right, waving his tomahawk all the while to convince the warrior he fully intended to use it. Then, when their horses were almost a yard apart, he turned his animal to the left, into Two Wolf's path, deliberately plowing his horse into the Arapaho's.

The animals collided with shattering impact. Nate had angled his horse just right, catching the warrior's mount on the point of its left shoulder. He Wolf's animal went down, but the warrior sprang clear before he could be pinned underneath.

Still astride his horse, Nate launched himself into the air, diving onto He Wolf as the man straightened and they both went down in a swirl of limbs. They separated and rose to their feet with their weapons at the ready.

There was a fierce gleam in He Wolf's eyes. "You are all they say you are," he said, and speared his knife at Grizzly Killer's throat.

Nate back-pedaled, his movements slightly restricted by the snow. The blade nicked his right wrist, drawing blood. He slashed with the tomahawk but He Wolf nimbly evaded the blow.

The Arapaho unleashed a flurry of stabbing and cutting strokes, pressing relentlessly, seemingly determined to end their fight quickly.

It took every vestige of energy Nate possessed to save himself from being ripped open. He blocked, countered, and thrust, his limbs a blur, sweat caking his skin, but he could do little better than hold his own. The sustained combat began to take its toll. On top of all he had previously been through, the injuries sustained, the long pursuit, and the series of fights, this final battle was proving almost too much for his battered, aching body to endure.

He was weakening fast, and from the smug smirk that creased He Wolf's lips, he suspected the warrior guessed it. In desperation he summoned his remaining strength and flailed away, seeking to batter the knife from the Arapaho's grip. But He Wolf danced rearward, staying just out of range.

Nate tripped. One moment he was swinging the

tomahawk for all he was worth, the next his left
moccasin gave way on the slick snow and he fell to his
knee.

Instantly He Wolf pounced, sweeping his knife
down at the white man's upturned face.

Frantically Nate brought the tomahawk up and
managed to deflect the blade. In a burst of inspiration
he perceived that he was employing the wrong strate-
gy. Instead of concentrating on warding off the knife,
he should be trying to get the man *wielding* the knife.
So as the Arapaho elevated the blade for yet another
stab, Nate sank the tomahawk into the man's left leg.

He Wolf arched his spine and involuntarily cried
out, then staggered backwards.

Nate yanked the tomahawk out and rose. He had
the upper hand and wasn't about to relinquish it. His
arm whipping right and left, he drove the warrior
farther and farther backwards. So engrossed was he
in trying to defeat He Wolf that he failed to register
the drumming sound of hooves until the horse making the noise was almost upon him. Then he glanced
around in alarm to find the warrior he had cut below
the ribs bearing down on him.

He Wolf shouted something in Arapaho.

Throwing himself to the right, Nate escaped being
crushed beneath the animal's powerful legs. He
landed on his side, then swept erect, his left hand
closing around his knife. If they were going to come
at him two at a time in violation of their agreement,
then he would face them with every weapon at his
disposal.

The mounted warrior checked his charge and
turned his horse. His hand was pressed over his
wound. Blood coated his skin all the way down to his
toes.

Waving his arms, He Wolf yelled at the warrior,
apparently trying to stop the man from attacking, but
his words were wasted.

Leaning to the right, then the left, barely able to grip the reins, the wounded Arapaho goaded his horse forward once again.

Nate tensed and crouched, prepared to leap either way to evade those pounding hooves. To his astonishment, He Wolf suddenly stepped between the onrushing warrior and himself and faced the animal.

The other Arapahos were shouting and converging at a gallop.

Confused, Nate saw He Wolf raise an arm in an effort to signal the young brave to stop. But the gesture was futile. The galloping horse bore down on He Wolf, who attempted to dodge to the left; his injured thigh caused him to stumble instead, and a heartbeat later the horse slammed into He Wolf and flattened him under its driving hooves. Nate heard a crackling and a crunching sound and blood spurted from He Wolf's mouth.

"Nate! Behind you!" Winona cried.

He whirled, and there were the two remaining warriors bearing down on him, one with a tomahawk, another with a war club. There was fury in their eyes and neither gave any indication of stopping.

A rifle boomed. The Arapaho holding the tomahawk stiffened and fell.

Nate knew Winona had fired. He drew back his knife arm, and when the last warrior came close enough he hurled the weapon with all the strength left in his body. He didn't expect to score, merely to force the warrior to turn aside, but to his astonishment the blade sped true and buried itself to the hilt in the Arapaho's chest. The warrior let go of his reins, clutched at the hilt, and toppled soundlessly.

Inhaling raggedly, Nate surveyed the battlefield.

The badly wounded warrior had stopped fifteen feet away. He sagged, his eyelids fluttering, then vented a groan and fell. After twitching for a moment, he was still.

None of the other Arapahos were moving.

Suddenly he heard footsteps behind him and spun, thinking one of the warriors had somehow revived and was attacking him. Instead, Winona was a yard away, the smoking Hawken in her right hand. She threw herself into his arms and they embraced, her robe parting as they pressed together, enabling him to feel her heart beating wildly. "Husband," she said tenderly. "Husband."

Nate simply held her, his face nestled in her flowing hair, and fought to prevent a flood of tears from overflowing his eyes. A lump formed in his throat. He tried to speak but couldn't. She was safe and in his arms and nothing else mattered.

For the longest time they stood there, immobile, glued to one another, as one in the midst of the vast wilderness, their bodies bathed in the golden sunshine.

Epilogue

Nate and Winona rode side by side on their own horses, winding down into their valley, their cabin beckoning to the east. He held the lead to the pack animals in his left hand. Cradled in his right arm was the Hawken.

Winona held a Kentucky rifle in her arms. She frequently glanced at her mate when he wasn't looking and grinned. "What will you do with all the guns?" she asked at one point.

"I don't rightly know," Nate replied thoughtfully. "We'll bury the crates near the cabin for the time being. They should keep for a while. I'll ask Shakespeare's advice the next time we see him."

"Just so we get rid of them. They are bad medicine."

They came to a clear stretch and a doe bounded from their path.

"Our baby is well despite all we have been through," Winona commented. "In three moons we will have a new addition to our family."

"I can hardly wait."

Winona gazed toward the cabin and glimpsed the horse pen. The sight made her chuckle.

"What's so funny?" Nate asked.

"I was thinking of the four hundred and twenty-two beaver pelts you have buried under the ground in the pen."

"What about them?" Nate inquired. With all that had been going on, he'd forgotten about the furs he'd collected during the last trapping season. As did most trappers, he'd cached his catch until the next rendezvous at which time he would pack them to the annual get-together and sell them for a hefty profit.

"Isaac Kennedy would have given anything to know about them."

"Kennedy was a fool. He never should have ventured out here. Some people have no business being in the wild," Nate said. After a bit he added, "I guess that old saying is true."

"What saying?"

"A man should always know his limitations."